The White Rose

Grace

ISBN: 978-1515272366 (sc)

Graphics Credits:
    Star photos on cover and page 8: Akira Fujii
    White rose: used under license from Shutterstock.com
    Author's photo: Bruce Polak
    Page 4: Puka, CC0
    Page 6: Venus and Sirius by the lake, Tunc Tezel
    Page 9: Hieroglyph of Sirius, Aaron Rose
    Page 56: Full moon over the Pacific, Public Domain
    Page 58: Sunlight on water, CC0
    Page 94: Venus over the Pacific, Brocken Inaglory
    Page 114: Falcon soaring, used under license from
    Shutterstock.com
    Page 116-117: Milky Way over Mt. Shasta,
    Goldpaint Photography

Book Editing, Design, and Layout by Aaron Rose,
Mount Shasta, California

Published by The Starlight Foundation Press

Grace can be reached at: corazondelsol@snowcrest.net

To the Sacred and Holy Mystery of Love…
and its full flowering
within every human heart.

And to the Divine Light of the One,
seeded at the dawn of Time.

Contents

Preface

There is a love not of this world…
but in rare moments, like some fine ethereal light
it may be glimpsed here…
As the brightest Eveningstar
that in the silvery hush of twilight
reveals her jewel-like radiance
ever so briefly
before slipping over the edge of darkness…

I remember when you came to me in the night
and shone your love through the light of the stars,
but too swiftly passing, you were gone.
Like the Eveningstar, you were here…then gone.

Introduction

The great star Sirius is the brightest amongst all the stars in the heavens ~ like a sparkling blue sapphire, its radiance illumines the darkness of the longest winter nights. All who gaze upon its shimmering beauty are touched in some deep and mysterious way, though they may not know why. But those few who do know, and they are few indeed, hold a sacred and mysterious secret in the depths of their hearts. To them it is not merely a star...

And so it is for these mystic dreamers that this story is written.

And although the mysteries of Sirius are too unfathomable to speak of, throughout the ages there have been those who have tried. Many ancient cultures have encoded the knowledge in monuments of stone, veiled in symbols, if not in words.

But perhaps it is in the hearts of lovers and dreamers that the truest knowledge is held, deep in the archives of the soul where are imprinted from the very beginning of this world the secret records of our origins.

Perhaps you are one who remembers...

 Hieroglyph of Sirius

Yes, myriad are the myths that surround the beautiful blue star. It is said that more than a few of the ancient mysteries of Egypt are entwined with Sirius, and this is true also in other cultures as well. From the deserts of Africa to the high Andean mountains, people have looked to this star with longing and listened to its song sing to their souls.

Some ancient peoples know it as the origin of the whales and dolphins, those extraordinarily conscious creatures who now inhabit our watery blue planet. Others say it is the Christ Star, the very one that the wise men followed to find the newborn messiah, whose birth was heralded in the heavens. And yet a few know Sirius to be the star of the Goddess, the celestial portal of the Cosmic Mother, whose unified consciousness of Infinite Love creates and guides the destiny of our souls.

To be sure, Sirius is a stargate ~ an interdimensional portal from the realms of pure formless light into this universe of form.

But above all, Sirius is a stunningly brilliant shining star ~ a sun beyond our sun…actually, it is two suns together, which are said to orbit about one another in a sacred dance…spiralling in a pattern much like the double helix of our human DNA. Could it be that we are woven of the same star stuff…intricately patterned after our original Homeland?

And could it be that long ago the first beings on this world were from Sirius and that they had come here in the beginning to seed a higher consciousness of exquisitely pure and Divine Light…?

Chapter 1
In the Beginning

Once upon a timeless time
there was a love...

a love not of this world, for it began far beyond this world and was brought here at the dawn of time.

This is a story about that love ~ how it came to be here and about how it was lost...once...and then again. And then again. Yes, it is a story about love lost but also found...and then lost once more and again found.

It is a story that has no real ending, as no true love story ever does; there are just pauses, the way the day pauses to give way to the night and then returns with the dawn.

Just cycles of time, appearing and disappearing, but never ending. Like the ebb and flow of tides, nothing ever really ends. Nothing that is true, that is...nothing of the heart.

When did this love begin; when does any love ever begin? It seems it was always there, just waiting behind the veils of time to be found again.

When first she looked into his great blue eyes, she saw it, though she didn't yet understand what it was. He was young, just entering the early summertime of his life, and she was nearing her autumn. In this culture, in this time, such a difference in years would be reason enough to keep the door of love closed, at least romantic love. And thus she entertained no such notion.

And yet...there it was...this unmistakable feeling that arose in her heart, a sort of recognition, that was both mysterious and yet wholly familiar.

He was young, but he bore a wisdom far beyond his years. She saw in his eyes a light; in truth it was more a luminous passageway...a passageway that took her far from this world, all the way back to the stars.

And she recognized something...and she remembered...something...she could not name. She could only feel her heart touched with an overwhelming tenderness. And there arose from within her an intense desire to serve his light in any way she could, to help him shine, to fan the embers of his soul fire.

Only much later would she realize that she was to be his initiator and awakener of ancient memories and celestial star codes.

It was the most unlikely meeting. Through the swirling white veil of a January blizzard he came walking into her life.

It was deep winter, and the snows had been falling relentlessly. She normally would be gone away during this season, off to the warmer lands, the sunlit isles, where she went each winter to swim with wild dolphins in the open seas. But a strange illness had overcome her, a sort of fever, that rendered her nearly delirious and certainly unable to leave her bed.

Long were the stormy hours and days she had lain feverish and aching, whilst the cold, white snows fell incessantly. This malady had the effect of causing her to feel more extraordinarily open and sensitized than usual, as though her skin were no longer covering her nerves, and everything felt excruciatingly heightened. Colours, sensations, feelings…all so heightened that her tears would flow at the merest sight of a snowflake falling outside her window. All life seemed especially exquisite, poignant, and precious, as though its beauty were almost unbearable to her senses.

One morning during this time of fever, she awakened to an intense feeling in her heart. It was a sort of ache that so gripped her that she clasped her hands over her chest and gasped with the sensation. Then she heard these words…in her mind, yet not her own…a mind now that was given over to listening to subtle vibrations far beyond thought. A Voice of infinite love and wisdom spoke through her, a Presence not of this world…

*"There is some rare and inexpressibly exquisite beauty
I long to bring into this world…"*

These words seemed to arise from her depths, as though her soul, unveiled and naked, pierced the veils of earthly density and spoke from the depths of silence. Catching this fragrance of soul, she closed her eyes and went deep within to seek the origin of this Voice. Deeper and deeper into her heart she penetrated, until it was so deep that she found herself seeming to go out the back of her heart as though it were a doorway, a doorway out into the stars.

Through this door she went, and out across the universe she journeyed, ever listening, ever seeking the source of this longing—the song of her soul and its origin. And as this trackless journey continued, deeper and deeper into the mystery of existence, the Voice continued…

"There is some rare and inexpressibly exquisite beauty
I long to bring into this world…

It lives behind my heart…far, far behind and beyond
out where the stars flicker, and further still

beyond the stars and whirling galaxies,
the myriads of worlds and suns and moons
beyond, beyond…
deeper and deeper into the dark mystery of space
to the other side of darkness and time and form

to regions beyond the mind's perceptions,
a distance incomprehensible, and yet
fathomed easily by the open innocence of the Heart.

Here at the point of origin,
in the silence beyond all sound,
and the light beyond all darkness
as in a pause before the first breath
that breathed all worlds into being
and long after the measure of time is no more,
This That I Am, Is…

a Love incomprehensible…
a Beauty unimaginable…
and yet
I would dream countless universes into being
in My attempt to express
My Heart…
My Heart…
My Heart…

My Heart that is more tender than a mother's,
for I Am the Mother of all mothers,
the Heart of all hearts,

the Breath of all breath
and the Beauty that shines through all beauty.

I cannot be named nor defined,
yet I define and re-define you,
create and re-create you
in My image,
each time your innocent heart is opened in love.

It is I longing for Myself who longs through you,
and the unutterably sweet mystery of our union
causes you to weep.

Your every tear is Mine
I created the stars thus...
and through your overflowing heart-waters
I pour into your world.
Surrender to My current...
Be overwhelmed, softened, and melted down
by the waves of feelings
flowing through your vulnerable heart.

It is I...entering your world as a tidal wave,
destroying all structures of time and mind
that cannot contain my unimaginable Love.

Relax...
surrender...
and be taken...
as gently as a leaf falling, or a tear
falling,
falling,
falling...
So am I
falling into you..."

As the words tumbled out into this world from some mysterious, unfathomable depths, she felt the invisible Presence of that One who is the origin of All…

That One she knew as Mother…the Great Mother of the world, Mother of the Universe. It was She who spoke from within her own small beating heart, as though her heart, and indeed all hearts, were created by Her with such infinite tenderness to be the very vessel through which She, the Creator, expresses into this world of form.

This longing for love, which she had felt so intensely all the days of her life, she now understood, as the Creator longing for Itself.

How beautiful, how poignant…and she understood this: that we are created to be the vessels for the One to know Itself.

In truth there is only One of us here…no me, no you, only the One longing for Itself.

And so we long for love, do we not? For She is That; we are That. All is That. As these exquisite feelings and revelations blossomed within her, she closed her eyes, savouring this moment of divine communion. And she remained in this deep silence for a very long time…

And as such, another day passed in this exquisitely open and otherworldly state she now was in, and as the descent of dusk fell once more upon the snow-covered earth, she fell again into a deep, dreamless sleep.

At last the fever subsided, and one morning she awoke, and though weak, she was determined to rise and begin to enter this world again. There was much she needed to take care of after being away so long.

She would make her way up the winding road that led from her little cabin in the woods to the place where she kept her car in the winter months, at the top of the hill. Up there, out of the hollow of the valley, there might be phone reception.

She was hoping that at last she was well enough that she could begin to set into motion her plans for travels to the warmer lands. Her longing was to be out of the snow. It seemed weeks had passed in this feverish delirium, and she wished to waste no more time. The warm oceans awaited, and her aching body longed for that comforting embrace of sea water and sunshine, and to be again with the wild dolphins.

Bundling up in winter coat, boots, gloves, and cap, to brave the storm, she sighed at how much trouble it is to be in cold weather. Wistfully she thought of the ease of warmer climes, where nearly no clothes were needed. *Soon, soon,* she thought.

Weak from her long sickness, she trundled up the snowy road that led to the upper area of the land, where the single highway wound its way up the mountain. All was white. White upon white...a blizzard of swirling snow enshrouding all the landscape. When at last she made it to her car parked up near the top, she climbed in, grateful to escape the falling snow and icy winds.

Sitting quietly for a time, regaining her breath from the walk up, she reflected that this was quite the storm, and it was crazy for anyone to be out in it, especially she who had been so sick that she hadn't even been able to get out of bed for weeks. But she must make some calls, try to book a flight, begin to make her travel plans.

She tried to make a call and found that there was no reception. It must be the blizzard, she thought, and surely the reception would return when the storm subsided. And so she decided to just sit quietly for a while and try again later. There was nowhere to go, no way to go, so she just surrendered to this being snowed in and cloistered from the world. She closed her eyes and leaned back in her seat, listening to the unutterable silence. It was, as always up here on this remote mountain, deafening.

After some time of sitting quietly, something moved her to open her eyes and turn her head to the left to look up the road toward the direction of where the buried highway lay. No one would be driving up this way today; even in fair weather few cars came up this remote road. For this she was glad, for she cherished the solitude and silence this remote place she lived offered.

Suddenly, through the swirling snows, she caught a glimpse of something. Was she imagining this…? A lone figure emerged out of the white mists of the storm and was making his way down the road toward her. She wondered who in the world would be out in this weather, way up here?

As she watched, puzzled, the figure drew closer and came right up to her window. She rolled it down, and as he pulled back the parka covering his face, she saw it was a young man. He said simply, matter-of-factly, "I was just passing by up on the road, and something made me stop. I felt there was something down here, something calling me, and I had to come down to see." He continued, "A few months ago I came up this road, and at this very same place I saw what looked like a twelve-foot-high pillar of light right in the middle of the road. Do you have any idea what this might have been?"

She was astonished, and intrigued by his question. And as she saw he was completely covered in snow, and shivering, she responded by saying, "Why don't you come around to the other side and get in out of the snow."

This he did, and when he was seated in the seat beside her he pulled back his hood and cap, all which were caked with snow. As he turned to look at her, a light came from his eyes that just took her breath away. It pierced her heart, and she was overcome by a feeling of profound recognition.

She could see he was young, maybe in his early 20's, of slight stature, with the most extraordinary blue eyes she had ever seen, and golden hair that hung damp around his neck to his shoulders.

His eyes were not eyes, they were burning windows. And as she gazed into their depths, she saw and knew and understood everything about him. "Have you always been this open?" she managed to stammer.

He just looked at her and shrugged. He told her he was going to school over near the coast and felt a call to come visit this mountain again, and though it was storming, he just had to come up here. He said he had been up here with a friend earlier in the season and they had both seen a beam of light right up there on the highway, right where he stopped again today. Did she know what it could be? he asked again, with great sincerity.

Thus they sat for the next timeless time, hours perhaps, who knows, and continued to share. When they had finished, he asked if he could come to see her again, that there was so much he wanted to ask her, so much he was seeking to understand. She replied that maybe he would like to come again in a few days, for tea. He could just come by then if he felt to, and she left it at that. Three days later, on Sunday afternoon, he came knocking on her door.

19

Some years before, she had had a profound experience that had changed her life forever. Actually it was more than an experience; it was a total Awakening, a mystical Union with All That Is that changed the course of her life. It occurred spontaneously one night as she slept out under the stars on a remote cliff above the sea, along the central California coastline of Big Sur. It was winter then too, February, and she was making a two-day journey by car to visit her family in the south.

On that first night she found a quiet place to park along a remote cliff, in off the winding narrow road of that rugged and wild coastline. Here she would camp for the night and resume her journey to the south the next morning.

Exhausted from the long drive of that day, she fell into a deep sleep, lulled by the haunting sound of the ocean waves far below the cliff where she lay.

In the late hours of the night she was awakened, suddenly. There was an overwhelming feeling that a light was shining fully upon her. She opened her eyes, bewildered, a bit confused in her between waking and sleep state, somehow expecting to find someone there who must be shining a flashlight or a lantern upon her.

But there was no one there…all was dark and quiet, but for the song of the waves crashing upon the cliffs far below, and above her were only the stars in the vast expanse of darkness.

No longer sleepy, but very awake now, she gazed up at the magnificent display of stars, all shining as crystalline jewels in the clear, cold winter night's blackness, above the dark, droning sea. There was no one there…only the stars, only the sea…

Her gaze fixed upon one star in particular, the brightest one in all the sky. Like a glittering diamond tinged with flashing blue, the star hung suspended in the darkness of the night heavens. This star she knew well. This was the star she always watched since she was a child, since she was a young girl walking alone through many winter nights in the south.

This star was the one she always said was hers, even when she didn't know its name. It was her star; at least that's how, in her innocence, it always had seemed. From the time she was a child, when she gazed upon its shimmering beauty, it had felt like Home.

But finally after all these years she knew its name: Sirius. And she loved this star beyond all the stars, though she loved them all. This star would always follow the processional of stars that she fondly knew as intimately as family or dear friends: the hunter Orion, whose belt of stars looked like a great kite, who chased the little Fox, who in turn chased the Seven Sisters. They all danced across the winter night sky in this shining processional that appeared in late autumn and disappeared over the horizon by springtime, to be gone to the south altogether in the summer.

Summer nights brought out new characters, but these never did captivate her in the same way as these old friends of the winter night sky. In her youth, she had spent many nights walking in the hills and valleys where she'd grown up, troubled by the world and seeking solace in her solitary wanderings and starry communions. When the world wearied her soul, she could disappear into the night, alone, sometimes not returning until the dawn. The light of day often felt too harsh, too brash and merciless. But the night was a soft blanket of tenderness that enfolded her sad heart and soul.

Why was she so sad? She did not even know. It was a certain feeling she had always had, a sort of homesickness and longing that had always haunted her. Where was home? She did not know, but nothing of this world felt like home.

Now this night, upon this wild remote cliff above the sea, she was awakened by the light of her star. Yes, something in its light that night carried a definite presence. She was transfixed as she lay there gazing at its radiance.

And then, quite extraordinarily, she began to be aware of an unusual sensation…a subtle yet distinctly clear sense of expansion, as though she were growing larger and larger and the spaces between her cells seemed to be moving further apart.

Out, out, out…she felt her awareness moving, expanding, becoming spacious. This feeling intensified, and with it an increasingly profound sense of expansion in her heart and mind that felt inexpressibly blissful. She had never before felt such bliss, and it kept expanding, in waves and waves and waves of ecstasy, as the song of the ocean's waves far below echoed through the chilly, still night air.

Now she was becoming so large, so wide, so expanded…she was becoming the vastness of space itself, moving out amidst the stars, moving out across the universe, wider and wider…until at last she was none other than the universe itself. She disappeared into everything; became the stars and sky, the crashing waves, the vast dark sea, the silent sleeping Earth that stretched out into the darkness.

She was no more who she had been, yet she was the most truly herself she had ever been; no separate self remained, only this sense of being One infinitely vast Being who was everything, everywhere, all at once.

Time stopped…there remained only an Eternal Now. All sense of space disappeared; she was everywhere, and everywhere was Here, Now. She was everything and beyond everything. She was One, the One. The One that alone Is. And this One was Infinite Love, a love so immense that all earthly ideas of love completely paled in meaning before its grandeur, as though what we know of love is but the merest drop, and this was an infinitely immense Ocean.

She was Awake; the One she had always sought, she Was. There was nothing else. No two. And for the first time in her troubled young life, the constant longing and yearning and seeking for something…for God, for Home, for love…ceased.

It was the cessation of all seeking, yes. A stillness and fullness and wholeness of Being that no words can describe. Ecstasy, bliss…beyond even these. And so full was this ecstasy that only tears could express it. Tears poured down her face, flowing like crystalline streams, flowing like luminous liquid Love from the Heart of the Eternal One.

How long she lay like this cannot even be guessed. For all sense of time had stopped, as she lay in the timeless embrace of Eternity.

Somehow that night passed, though she has no memory of its passing. She does not remember the coming of the morning and how the day unfolded. Somehow she must have gotten again behind the wheel of the car, for the first recollection she had was of driving into Santa Barbara, some 200 miles to the south, later that afternoon. Her first awareness was that she was thirsty. Very, very thirsty.

So, as she came into the town she searched for a market where she might find some water. She remembered only that it felt very strange to walk into that store, that she found it difficult even to walk at all, and that everything seemed foreign and unfamiliar, as though she had just arrived from another planet.

Disoriented, feeling in an altered state, she did not remember the night before and what had occurred. But she somehow was able to continue her journey on for another hour, up into the hills of the Ojai valley, where she was expected by her dear friends.

A year passed, with no recollection of that night beneath the stars upon a lonely cliff above the droning sea of the Big Sur coast. But one winter morning, one year later, in a completely unexpected way, it all came back to her...

***

It came first as a sensation upon the top of her head, a sort of fluttering touch, as though there were wings above her. And then she began to feel the sense of expansion again, and the sensation that the cells of her body were beginning to move apart. Now there was more space between her cells; now she was becoming something very wide and vast, and she recognized this sensation. Sitting down, in meditation, she prepared herself for whatever might follow.

Then there came a Voice, melodic and sweetly familiar, speaking from within her own mind...or was it her mind? Whose mind, she could not tell. A Voice like a song, a song of exquisite beauty and purity, sung from beyond time and space, from beyond this world…

"If I could but speak to you the ancient Language of Light, you would weep with remembrance…" it began.

Who was this voice, so familiar, so true and deep and certain? She listened for more…and the Voice continued:

"But I have remained mute for oh, so long, that even I forgot my song."

She wrote these words in her little journal that lay beside her and listened for more.

"Lonely I have been upon this plane, deep has been my longing to go Home…and silent my voice from earthly sound, for once sang I a song not yet here found."

The beautiful, melodic words just kept flowing through her mind, tumbling out upon the paper as she wrote as fast as she was able to translate the vibrations of light into language…

"It was a simple language of Being…Light impulses conveyed through feeling…a subtle resonance of spirit echoing through cell and heart and soul, merging and re-emerging into the All…"

Still more came, swiftly and without faltering…

"Essence to essence we touched,
and spoke the silent language of the stars,
mirroring through our eyes and hearts
the Light of who we are…
for we were One, and knew not what it was to be alone.

Ours was a realm of purest love,
innocent and infinitely sweet,
we breathed the fragrant breath of God,
hearts pulsing as one, within the One heartbeat…
If I sing to you the star name of Sirius,
does your soul begin to hear an ancient song?
Of dimensions beyond the stars and suns,
angelic spheres of radiance
within the body of the Infinite One?
It is that One, alone, who speaks through all that is…
rise up my children, come Home, return to blessedness.
Now the light of the stars and sea awakens also in me,
the ancient memories etched within my cells,
and the song of the Eternal One,
in truth I have always sung,
for it is the very essence of who I am…
only now I am remembering, and singing it again…"

And thus the first of what would be two years of ongoing poetic transcriptions poured through her that day. They would come at any hour, day and night, sometimes waking her from her sleep, but always preceded by that soft fluttering touch upon her crown and the familiar melodic Voice beginning once again…

When he came knocking on her door that winter morning, three days after their first meeting, she greeted him politely and invited him up to her little sanctuary. The snows had stopped falling, but the air was icy and the sky a pewter grey. Great mounds of deep snow lay all around.

She made tea, and they sat for a time sharing a few words of introduction. The fire was burning and crackling, and the warm air enfolded them in a welcome blanket of comfort.

He told her he was in school, university, as he had mentioned before, but he was disillusioned with it all. After finding the mountain for the first time a few months before, he just kept feeling called to return. There was a restlessness in his soul, and coming to the mountain was medicine. The schooling was for his family, he confessed. It was expected of him. But he was looking for something more...

He was a bit shy, and found few words, and this she found endearing. It was in his eyes that she heard and saw all that she needed to know. Remarkably, she found herself telling him things she never, or rarely, if ever, told anyone. She spoke about the stars, especially the one star she knew as her own. Somehow, the words just tumbled through her, as though she were downloading a message that had been destined to be delivered to him from some long-distant time. She just let it come through, and he only listened, his great blue eyes growing wider as she spoke.

When at last they parted, she wondered at herself. What on earth was she doing? Why had that all come through like that? Had he comprehended any of it, or just thought her crazy?

One week later he called her again, this time from the coast where he was going to school. He said he was going to be passing through the area in a few days, going north to visit family, and could he stop in to visit again? She said yes, and invited him to come join the birthday gathering that would be happening on her behalf the very night that he would come. She said it would go late, and if he wished he could stay the night in her spare room as well, before continuing his journey the next morning.

She did not like celebrating her birthday. She dreaded it. She never had related with time, and so to celebrate its passing seemed so strange to her, yet friends were making special efforts to honour her. She, on her part, secretly wished that she was far away, where no one knew her, passing that day quietly alone. Or with dolphins. But as the sickness had kept her from travels, she had surrendered to this fate and agreed to have this birthday celebrated with dear friends. A social person she was not…in fact, social events pained her, especially if they focused upon her. But her friends she loved dearly, and it was a source of great joy for them all to celebrate her birth into this world.

She secretly had always thought, perhaps wistfully, that she would not live so long in this life. The world had always wearied her, and she had been Homesick for as long as she could remember. Except for that one night… some years before…when she had lain beneath the luminous stars, beside the singing sea…and gone Home.

So, the gathering happened in the evening, and it was indeed a time of beauty and joy and love shared by all. She danced and laughed and rejoiced in how blessed she was to have such wonderful friends as these. Her young, new friend came back with her, and as was planned, slept in the spare room.

In the morning, they shared tea and sat for a while out in the crisp morning air in a little sheltered corner deck that faced south and gathered a bit of the warmth of the pale winter's morning sun. He spoke of his disillusionments again, with school, with society. He wanted to quit school, but the pressures from his family were keeping him from doing this, at least for the time. They seriously thought that something was wrong with their son. Maybe he was on drugs, they had surmised. Maybe he needed to see a therapist? His feelings of disillusionment and the accompanying misunderstandings this provoked in his family weighed heavy upon his heart.

As she listened intently to his concerns and felt more deeply into his being, her heart was stirred with feelings of tenderness and empathy. She felt an overwhelming sense of wanting to protect him, and to take him under her wing. She also felt a deep desire to help him to cultivate his spiritual development, for she could see that he already carried such a pure light, and this urge to help fan the embers of his soul suddenly overcame her.

She had been a spiritual mentor to many, a teacher and healer who had devoted all of her life to the awakening of humanity and the upliftment of consciousness, particularly the healing of the heart and our human experience of separation.

Thus these feelings came naturally to her, but she did notice they were especially potent in regards to him. There was something…different. Something so familiar; it was as though she had known him before. Yes, unmistakably, that was it. And as she let this awareness rise up within her, she was astonished at how deeply her heart responded to him. Who was this mysterious young man who had just wandered into her life in such an unlikely way?

As he prepared to go on his way, she pondered these things. She walked him up the long driveway to where his old truck was parked, next to hers, up closer to the road where it was easier access through the snow. The pale winter sun shone upon them as they walked and shared. She told him that she was preparing to leave soon for the remainder of the winter, to the islands, to swim with wild dolphins.

It surprised her that she revealed this to him, as she usually kept her life and affairs very private and told little to anyone. Especially of her whereabouts. But what happened next surprised her even more. In fact, it completely astonished her. Before she even had time to think about it, she found herself extending an invitation to him to come join her, at any time, to swim with the dolphins, if he felt moved.

After they had parted, and he had driven away, she shook her head in amazement. What had she just done? She could hardly believe it. This was so unlike her. She was such a private person and so valued her solitude; she protected it at all costs. Yet, when she felt into her heart, there it was…she knew she had had no other choice.

Well, anyway, it was unlikely that he would come.

But he did come. Some weeks after she had already been in the islands, he called her one day. Could he come in a week or so, he asked? He said he'd left school, temporarily, or at least that is what he'd assured his family. He just needed a break. And he had taken a job, in those weeks since he had seen her last, that had afforded him the funds to make the journey.

And so it happened that this young man, whom she hardly knew, and yet she felt she knew deeper than she could comprehend, came to be her companion in the warmer lands, to swim with her and the wild dolphins in the healing seas.

In the weeks to follow, they shared a sweet, innocent comradeship, enjoying the golden sunlit days together, the shining sea, sweet fruits, the simple joy of life. As children in the garden they played. They swam with the wild dolphins in the open ocean and shared the exquisitely awakened Presence that these supremely conscious creatures of the sea embodied. These she considered her teachers, and it brought her great joy to introduce him to them.

And there continued to be this deep thread of desire in her heart to help him to blossom in his fullest light. So she found she wanted to take him to any conscious person she knew, expose him to every teaching and practice she had ever been blessed by, and touch his heart with the light of consciousness. And so it was.

He stayed with her in the islands for some weeks, and then went his way. It would be a while before they would meet again…

Time passed, a year or more. He would come and go from the mountain from time to time, but she heard from him seldom. He was exploring and searching, looking for himself. As if dreamwalking, oblivious to the deeper destiny unfolding, they each went their own way.

She was feeling time's passage, lonely and Homesick, even as she had always been, it seemed, for so much of this life. He was off exploring the worldly things of the human dimension and finding little there that nourished or fulfilled his heart's longing.

The time was passing…and ripening…for their meeting once again in a whole different dimension of the heart.

Never would she have imagined what was to unfold.

Another season passed, and even as the wild geese who migrate to the warmer lands with the coming of winter, she too once more made her migration to the south. He had in the autumn time moved to the mountain, finally making clear to his family that school was not where he wanted to be. She saw him only occasionally, and he stayed upon the mountain through that winter season. The raw and powerful energy of the mountain was working his soul, clearing and purifying him of much of his past.

In the quiet depths of each of their hearts there was a longing...for what? They were lonely, yes...isn't that the way of this human realm? So it has always seemed. This she had accepted. Hadn't this been much of the fuel that had set her upon her lifelong spiritual journey? God alone, spirit alone, could fill that space, she reasoned.

But they did not yet glimpse what was to come nor understand its implications. How could they know that nothing could fill that secret and sacred place in their hearts that only they were to fill for each other? How could they know that God was here, incarnate in these very forms, awaiting to be awakened within the depths of the most tender and innocent human love?

It was not until the early springtime, when the streams were gushing with melting snows and new life was arising in the earth, that they met again. It was more than two years since their first meeting, when he had wandered through the blizzard and into her life.

It was arranged that he would meet her at the airport as she returned from the islands. He was there, with a single white rose in his hand. In a playful jest, he bent his knee and presented her with the rose, pledging his service as her knight to ever serve her. He playfully quipped that his steed awaited outside to carry her back to her castle.

As they drove back through the darkness of that spring evening, they spoke of many things, their journeys and experiences since they'd seen each other last, and it seemed that no time had passed. This comfortable, easy feeling of being together just was there as always.

It had been raining for weeks, he said, but perhaps when there was a break in the weather they might go for a walk together out by the lake? And so a few days later, when the rains had subsided, they did. They walked across the rain-drenched meadows, beside streams swollen and singing with snowmelt, beneath the grey rain-laden skies.

It was playful and joyful, as always...and both felt drunk on the sweet wine of springtime and the budding flower of innocent love they felt in their hearts. They danced and laughed and were utterly silly, like two children. He lifted her up and carried her across the wet lands, across the rushing rivulets, and would deposit her on dry ground again, with a knightly gesture of a bow. "At your service, my lady..." and they would laugh and playact like this.

They walked quietly for a time, along the river and into the forest. Then stopping for a moment, he suddenly bent forward and touched his brow to hers. It was a deep gesture of listening and communing with one another beyond any words. And something stirred in her heart... something so familiar and deep, as ancient memories were ignited in her soul.

What is this? she wondered, startled by the intensity of the feelings which seemed to confuse her mind, but not her heart. It was as though their souls were calling to one another, a long-lost song echoing through corridors of time, ever drawing them nearer, a destiny moving them, as certain as the relentless tides.

***

The springtime blossomed into summer, and she returned from another journey, this time to Europe. She often toured there in the springtime, offering her healing work and teaching, touching the weary hearts of a hurting world.

She had most recently been to the south of France, in the Languedoc region, near the border of Spain. Here she had visited the ancient ruins of a place called Montsegur. It was a castle high upon a rocky precipice in a most beautiful part of that mountainous region. As she walked amongst the ruins, she reflected on the story of what this place had once been.

The last stronghold of the Cathars, she was told. The Cathars…she had heard of them, but knew very little. They were a sect of gnostic Christians who were known for their purity and simplicity and their healing powers.

But the Church in power felt they defied all orthodoxy and, threatened by their pure demonstrations of Christ-like lives, had them sought out and destroyed. After scouring all of France for these heretics, it was here at Montsegur the last remaining Cathars were found by the soldiers of the Inquisition. They bravely had held off the assaults of the soldiers through a long, harsh winter, undefended, save for their pure hearts and the light that carried them through all darkness.

Finally they were forced through sheer exhaustion and starvation to come down off the rocky clefts and their crumbling, besieged fortress that had given them a remnant of refuge all those long, cold winter months. And so, arm in arm, two hundred brave and noble Cathar souls walked down that mountainside in the early spring of that terrible year and threw themselves into the fires of the Inquisition.

As she walked silently down that same mountainside, some seven hundred years later, she reflected on their plight. And it seemed that she could almost feel herself there…yes, the images seemed strangely clear and familiar…but she shook her head to shake off that sad and painful flight of her fancy.

Some weeks later, she returned home from the south of France to her own mountain and her little remote sanctuary. She always felt cloistered here in the silence and solitude this humble abode offered her. The world was wearisome to her; she ventured out only to serve the suffering of humanity, then took refuge here again. This is what she had been doing for many years; actually in one way or another this is what she had done this whole lifetime. Yes, she was a hermit by nature, but she was also a healer, by birth, and a lover of life, and she deeply felt the pangs of the human condition and could not do other than offer what she could to ease them.

But this return from being out in the world was different. She had made this journey to Montsegur… and the rarefied air of an ancient memory had breathed into her veins. The song of the Brotherhoods, the noble Pure Ones, was awakened in her heart. And she was beginning to remember…

They met again, and this time the fruit of their meeting was ripe... One warm twilight of a summer's eve, he came and found her in her garden. She was amidst the flowers and vegetables, picking supper. Her heart was heavy and troubled with feelings she did not understand.

But he came, and as though his feelings were inseparable from hers, he spoke what had been for so long unspoken...the words his heart had longed to speak, and hers had longed to hear.

He professed his undying love to her there, in the dusky fading light; he spoke with an unmistakable power that astonished her, and she recognized a truth so pure and deep that all the shadows of doubt paled before such clear light. It was as if all time stopped, and they entered another realm of being, a luminous realm where love alone prevails. And she felt and heard his heart, unveiled now from all hesitation and fear...

"I have waited for you forever..."

One kiss, more innocent than the flowers in her garden and as intoxicating in its beauty; one kiss, only that...and she was lost to this world, swept away in a torrent of feelings that had waited untold ages to be felt.

Chapter 2
The Pure Ones

In the southern mountainous regions of a land now known as France, there are ancient secrets held in the earth and in the stones, of a time long ago…

In that sacred land a seed of Light was planted.

Here is where the remnants of the holy family of the Anointed One had passed, in exile from their homeland along the Dead Sea. The Light of that one known as Messiah was carried through the holy women who had been nearest him, to this distant land. Here the essence of His Shining was imbued into the secret Orders that were formed to hold and protect this precious Light.

From the ancient lineage of the Essenes, this seed took root and sprang forth to later become those known as "the Pure Ones," the gnostic Cathars. These Pure Ones lived and held sacred the perfect truths that Yeshua had brought to this world. They followed the pure ways of Christ as they walked amongst the people, robed in simple white, and offered themselves in service to all in pure Christ-like love and brotherhood.

But the arising Christianity and its church, created to embody and exemplify His teachings, was instead threatened by the pure simplicity and truth the Cathars reflected. The church feared the truth.

A command was put forth from the hierarchy of Rome that all Cathars be tried for Heresy. They were sought out, questioned, and given the choice to forsake their heretical ways and convert to the Church or be burned at the stake.

But the Cathars were deeply devoted to their faith; thus few or none would convert. Having not the fear of death, they believed in Eternal Life and in the pure lands of soul to which they would go upon leaving this world. And thus the fires of the Inquisition burned fiercely across the land, and many innocent Pure Ones were put to death.

Long before even the Inquisition had begun, it was surmised by the wise ones of the Brotherhoods that distortion of the pure Christ teachings would happen. Alas, had it not always been so? Such was the way of the unawakened consciousness upon this planet that Christ himself had come to redeem.

They understood that the Light was a pure seed, and a seed once planted requires time for its germination and growth. As such, it must be protected at all cost until that time when it is come to full flowering and fruition. Thus, secret orders were established to keep hidden and protected the precious pure Christ Light that had been seeded here so long ago.

One Order in particular was created solely for this purpose. The Order of the White Rose was established and secreted away in the rocky clefts and hidden catacombs of that mountainous region. So secret it was that none amongst even the Cathars spoke its name, and thus it remained completely unknown, unseen and protected.

The Knights Templar were aligned with the Cathars in that they deeply recognized and honoured the unmistakable Christ-like essence that the "Bon Homme" embodied. They pledged their service in protection of the Pure Ones, and many wealthy lords of the land opened their castles as sanctuaries and places of refuge for the besieged Cathars. They valued the spiritual presence and pristine teachings these simple followers of Christ offered.

So it was that the Cathars, the Bon Homme, the good people of Christ, who had lived in such utter simplicity and poverty, asking nothing but to serve Love in the footsteps of their Lord, came to be cloistered away in grand castles perched high upon the rocky precipices.

Within one of these castles, or rather shall we say beneath, in the hidden chambers and catacombs that were most protected, there was kept secreted the most precious of all treasures: The White Rose.

This most sacred Order consisted of twelve Knights Templar who kept vigilant guard over the treasured pure Christ essence that was represented and embodied in a young Priestess. She was the White Rose. She was the one who held and carried the purest vibrations of Light, that had been transferred down through the lineages of Light, going all the way back to the time of Christ Yeshua, and even before. These Light Codes were brought here to this world at the dawn of Time, from beyond this world. These were the seeds of Light that would, once planted in the human dimension, begin to transform and awaken human consciousness into the flowering of a luminous race of Divine Beings.

These held the blueprints for the Christing of this planet.

She was the White Rose. More innocent and fair than the whitest rose, indeed. She was a Priestess of the Lineage of Light which had come to this world at its very beginning, through the stargate of Sirius to Venus, and then after much preparation and alignment of energies, to Earth. The far denser vibrations of Earth required a certain stepping down of frequency, from the higher spheres to this deepest and most challenging realm.

In her lineage, all who had come before had made this direct passage, each one carrying a certain fragment of the Christ Light that was to be seeded within the daunting density of Earth. This was the mandate from the Councils of the Christ within the Sun of Sirius. Earth was a troubled and lonely world, far out in the outer arm of the Milky Way Galaxy, remote from its Solar Source. But it held great potential. It had all the right conditions for life in a dimension far lower than either Sirius or Venus could offer. Its perfectly placed distance from its Sun allowed for physical life in the third dimension to occur.

This was very intriguing to the higher dimensional beings of Sirius. The idea that perhaps with care and time (oh, yes, Time…that strange phenomenon that occurred only in the third dimension!) the higher vibrational frequencies of Sirius could marry with the denser material vibrations of Earth to create something that had not yet been done…a race of Divine God Beings incarnated in physical matter!

This idea was so compelling to the Sirians that after mulling it over for aeons (although in their realm of non-time it was only a moment) it was decided upon to send the first Starseeds and begin the grand experiment. And so it was from the very beginning of this world that the garden of Earth was planted with seeds of Light, intended to blossom into an enlightened race of physicalized God Beings.

She was known as Lumiere…the Luminous One, the Light. And this she was. If a star could be embodied in a human form, this would be her. Radiant and lovely as a star, a soft luminescence seemed to envelope her, touching all who might be blessed enough to be in her presence. But these were very few, as she was so secreted away that only those nearest her who cared for her needs had that blessing.

Hers was the task to simply remain in cloistered purity, protected from any outer influences that might taint the pristine essence of the One Light she was appointed to represent and hold. In truth, she was not so much chosen for this position as born into it, being of the lineage of Light holders that went all the way back to the beginning. It was this lineage that had first seeded the planet with Light from Sirius and throughout all the ages of Earth appeared again and again in various forms. Her soul had always held such a position; in other lives, in other worlds.

Before her incarnation on Earth she had been prepared in the temples of Venus, following the pathway of all the Christ lineage: from Sirius to Venus to Earth. The pure vibrations of Venus, the Love Star, yet pulsed within her cells, as well as the Solar Goddess energies of Sirius, and this it was that was needed to be kept pure and undistorted.

Hence she was cloistered away from the denser vibrations of Earth. Since her birth she had been always cloistered; she knew nothing else. Her world was the hidden chambers within and underneath the innermost depths of the castle, as well as a higher chamber that opened out into the fresh air and sunlight and the vast, sweeping panorama of the surrounding mountains and valleys. Up here she could go out into a secret garden and be with the elemental forces of earth and sky.

A little mountain stream flowed through this garden, as well, singing and laughing as it happily went its way down the mountainside. Thus she had all the elements here…the earth, sky, water, and the fire of the sun. It was understood from the ancient times that all the elements must be present and in balance for life to remain in wholeness and balance as well. From each of the elements she was taught the deepest mysteries.

In the ancient ways of her ancestors she communed with Nature, worshipping the Sun as Father, the fire of Life, and the water as our Mother, the womb of creation. For it is and was in the union of sunlight and water that all lifeforms came into being.

She would sit quietly, watching the sunlight dance upon the water as a million diamonds of brilliant white light. This she knew was our origin. We had come to this world so long ago, at the beginning when all was water, like this: as drops of Sunlight. We had come and touched this world first with our Pure Light. Later the forms would be created, but first it was the Light upon the waters.

Those moments she had in the clear, pure air of those mountainous heights, gazing forever into the deep blue sky and the golden white radiance of the Sun, communing with the shining waters, were the most ecstatic in her young life. And at night she exalted in the vast starry heavens, lying sometimes for hours upon the earth, looking deep into the firmament. These were her companions...the stars, the sun and moon, the waters, the winds, and the soaring birds that flew overhead and sometimes came to land on her outstretched hands. Oh, how she loved them all! Her days were filled with the simple, pure wonder of life. And these communions with Nature and the elemental forces were her teachers.

She was not taught the skills of man...neither to read nor write, nor even to speak much. She was left to be in silence and solitude most of the time, and as such, her mind was kept uncluttered with the usual chatter of those minds that have been overfilled with learning. She came to know what was essential, and this of her own accord: to gaze into the stars and sun and feel one with all eternity, to listen to the silence and to the beating of her own heart, and to follow the flow of her own breath arising and falling as waves of the sea.

She learned to observe the perfect cycles of Nature and the seasons, the movement of the stars and moon across the heavens, and the ability to sit still for untold hours of timeless time, gazing deeply within and feeling the exquisite flow of light through her body.

She naturally felt only love, for she knew nothing else...this was her true nature, the true nature of all when left undefiled. She had no fear, for she had never been given reason to fear. She felt only a perfect sense of oneness with all existence. And this was her simple task: to Be. To Be the embodiment of pure love, undefiled by the fears and shadows that cover the Light of Being, as clouds that cover the sun.

In her simple and pure innocence, she held for this world a thread of Light, that kept the flame of Love's pure truth alive for all. For if only one upon this world remains in this undistorted consciousness, embodying

Love's Pure Light, then it will be sustained, though the darkness encompasses everywhere else. Thus she must be protected, she must…

And so the young years of her life passed, and when she was in the flowering fullness of her youthful radiant beauty, something happened that was to change everything…

Chapter 3
The White Rose

The Order of the White Rose consisted of twelve Knights who kept guard over the White Rose, the symbol of pure Christ Light. These were Templar Knights, in service to Christ, and in service to the Lords of the land. They, too, felt a deep alliance with the Cathars, recognizing the pristine principles of spiritual truth that these simple pure ones exemplified. Thus it was for these twelve a great honour and privilege to be in the service of this most secret and sacred Order.

Of these knights, there was one whose heart was the most golden. Golden like the sun and shining with a purity and light that only the sun could rival. The name he bore was Godone, the God one, the fair and noble one of God. He was golden-hearted, and golden was his hair, which cascaded down to his shoulders. His eyes were a piercing blue.

Neither he nor any of the knights of the Order had ever seen the White Rose; it was not permitted. But she lived in each of their hearts as the purest ideal and the highest expression of the truth and divinity that they served.

No, he had not seen her, none of them had. Perhaps she was just a dream, just a symbolic image…and so he longed to see her, he longed to know if she really existed. But how could this be? It was strictly forbidden.

And then it happened…but how it happened is not sure. Perhaps he climbed stealthily up the rocky precipices above her secret garden and quietly gazed down upon her there as she sat beside her little stream, communing with the light upon the water. Or perhaps he had hidden in some secret passage and had caught a glimpse of her as she was escorted from one of her chambers to another.

No, it is not known for sure, but what is sure is that this one glimpse burned deeply into his heart and would not let him rest. She was lovely beyond compare; the flower of youth was upon her, perhaps not more than 18 years of age, he guessed, although it could not be certain, for she also bore a dignity and depth that only one much older might have. Her long hair was golden, her form delicate, her face like that of an angel, and the light that shone about her was like that of the stars. A smouldering ember ignited in his depths. He was overcome by the desire to see her again.

But it was forbidden. He must not even think such things! Yet this burning desire would not leave him. Many were the long hours and days he struggled with these feelings. Yet he was passionate and untameable, and he had an especially wild streak in him as one who had lived the dangerous life of a knight and had grown accustomed to living on the edge of life and death.

And so it happened that one night, cloaked in the protective shrouds of a moonless darkness, he made his way to her hidden chambers.

***

It was in the late hours of the night, but she was not sleeping. She slept little, preferring to commune with the stars in the deep silence of the night. And this night she was out in her cloistered garden, sitting straight and silent, facing the east and the rising processional of stars that grace the winter night's sky. The air was cool and crisp, and she was cloaked in a white woollen cape, draped over her shoulders and down over her seated form. Softly illumined by the starlight, she looked like a flower seated there, a white lily, or more precisely, a white rose, with her petals arranged all around her.

Silently she gazed to the east, and over the rim of the mountains there arose a great shimmering star, alone in its brilliance, shining and flashing a blue-white fire.

He stood breathlessly in the shadows of the wall just behind her, watching her for some long while, and the star as it rose higher above the rim of the mountains just beyond her motionless form. And something inexpressible began to stir in his depths. Transfixed, as in a dream, images and feelings began to flood his awareness. And without realizing he had done so, he breathed a deep sigh. With this subtlest sound, she turned to glance behind her. Her eyes grew wide as she saw his dim form in the shadows, but she was not afraid. She knew he would come. She had been waiting...

⁂

She was a flower; as innocent and pure as the first blossoms of springtime. She knew nothing of the ways of the world, nor the ways of human love. But she was fearless in her utterly open vulnerability, and this touched his heart with a depth of feelings even more than already he'd felt. Her innocence was like the light of the stars, like the sunlight dancing on the waters, like the silvery silence of so many moonlit nights. He was breathless when he beheld her; she was startled, but unafraid, only open and curious, like a child.

47

But the recognition was immediate and unmistakable. She knew. And he knew, though he struggled with the immensity of this knowing. It was like worlds collapsed within him, and his mind blurred and dissolved as ancient, timeless memories flooded his heart. He just stood before her and stared. All time stopped, and for what seemed an eternity, they were lost in each other's gaze.

Then he held out his hand to her, his gaze never leaving her eyes. And like an innocent child, she took his hand, flushing with warmth as she did so. He gently pulled her to him and into his arms, and she nearly collapsed with the intensity of the energy. Her heart was swimming with feelings, he was beyond himself, and in this embrace they merged for a long time…and were lost to this world.

And so the night passed, and before the first light of dawn had flushed the sky, he slipped away, secretly leaving her chambers, with no one ever to know.

All through the days he could not bear it until the night came again, when he would once more steal into her chambers and into her embrace. And she, too, was lost in a timeless reverie, far away from this world, as the hours of the day passed until his return. And so it was that he came each night, in the secret darkness, unknown by any, to her chambers. And they would lie together and love through the night until the first hint of dawn hastened him away once more.

From the moment he slipped away, her heart ached and longed for him to return. And thus the days wore on until the evening, when she would listen breathlessly for his quiet footfall. And when he slipped through some secret entrance in the darkness and laid beside her, she felt as though all time stopped, and her heart melted into an infinite ocean of Love. In his arms she was Home; in her arms he found, at last, the only true resting place he'd ever known.

Of course, she had never known a man, a lover. She was indeed as naive and innocent as a flower. He was a knight, a traveller of many lands, carrying the musky essence of a worldlier life, of swords and shields and steeds and noble battles. Through him, she glimpsed and touched what she would otherwise never know. And through her, he also glimpsed and touched what he would otherwise not know: a shining world of spiritual light so pure and divine that it lifted his soul to lofty spheres far above the darkness of man's world. Quickening his soul, moving his heart to tears, his great blue eyes shone with the luminosity of who he now remembered himself to be. In her presence he remembered…Home.

<hr/>

Time passed, as it does in this strange world… one year and then another. Their secret love went unnoticed. He would appear and disappear according to the rhythms of his knightly callings. Sometime there were long spaces of time when he was away, called off to other lands and other duties. When he was gone, her heart ached unbearably. But when at last he would return, slipping quietly in beside her in the dark hours of the night, it was an ecstasy that no words can describe. And they would fall again into the timeless ocean where their souls merged. Their love-making was the divinely passionate fulfilment of two souls reunited into the One they really were.

Their love deepened; her pain at his absence came often, as he was called away more now, for the world was changing, and he was needed in faraway places. She feared he might not return…and alas, there came a time when indeed he did not…or when he did, it was too late.

The fires of the Inquisition were raging. The Cathars, the Bon Hommes, the Pure Ones, were being hunted and found in the secret places of the rocky mountains and taken by the soldiers of Rome to be burned as heretics of the Christian Church. Such irony! Those who bore the most pure and sacred truth of the One which the Church professed to follow, were destroyed. Their purity was too great a threat to the dark powers that be.

It became dangerous to stay where they were, and so it was determined that the Order should be moved further into the mountains, to a more remote region. There the White Rose, Lumiere, would be carefully escorted and secreted away.

Thus it was that in the darkness of a moonless night, Godone led her out through the secret passages to the horses waiting in the yard below. It was late summer, with the first hint of autumn in the air. A slight chill was in the night air, and he trembled as he hoisted his precious Lumiere up upon the back of the bay mare who stood patiently awaiting his command. Then, swinging himself up into his own saddle, he took the reins of her mare and led her out through the gates. All was quiet, but for the sigh of the wind in the trees and the distant call of an owl across the forest.

In the darkness, Lumiere turned once to look

back through the shadows to her beloved sanctuary. It would be the last time she would ever see those familiar walls that enclosed her home, the only home she had ever known.

Before dawn's light had illumined the landscape, they arrived at their destination. In the pale dusky twilight before dawn, the castle and fortress loomed ahead, high up on the rocky clefts of the mountainside at Montsegur. Here she would be given refuge, along with others of the Brotherhood who were fleeing in exile from their homes across the land. Godone led Lumiere's mare up the steep and narrow pathway to the fortress gate, and carefully helped her slip off wearily to the ground. From there he carried her inside and was met by several others of the Order, who guided him to an inner chamber where she would be cloistered. *She would be safe here, God willing,* he sighed and prayed silently under his breath.

There would not be time to stay with her; he must make haste and ride hard before the dawn's light made his movements too visible, toward the west where he would stand with other brothers of the Order in defence against any soldiers of the Inquisition who might come that way.

In the secreted chamber where she was taken, for a moment alone, he held her tight against his heart. She was so weary; she fell into his chest and sobbed.

"Be brave, my love," he said, "God is with you," and he raised her beautiful tearful face up to look once more deep into the dark pools of her eyes. "I will be back," he said. "And now you must rest and regain your strength." He kissed her lips once more and breathed in the fragrance of her hair and her essence that he loved and knew so well. "I will be back…" and he turned swiftly, so as not to show his own tears, and disappeared into the shadows that precede the dawn.

But he did not come back…and it seemed to Lumiere as though he were but a dream that had appeared in her life like a phantom and then had vanished again into the mists.

She was secluded away in the catacombs beneath the fortress, safeguarded from harm and the great darkness that would shadow their world. Yet she pined away for her beloved, her heart aching with missing him, and with deep, tearful concern she feared for his well-being. Had he been taken down in battle, lost to this life, and to her once again? Many were the nights she wept as she laid alone in the darkness. And many and fervent were her prayers for her beloved. *May he be safe; may he return again…*

But the late summer turned to autumn, and the winds of change began to blow. And soon enough, the autumn turned to early winter, and the first snows softly fell. And one morning, echoing across the valley below, a sound more cold and ominous than death came ringing through the frozen air. It was the clattering of many horses' hooves striking the stone pathways that led into the valley. The soldiers of the Church had come.

They set up camp down below, at the base of the mountain, whereupon the fortress and castle sat perched upon the rocky clefts high above. And here they stayed through that long, cold winter and began their siege upon the last remaining Cathars.

It was the longest and coldest winter, indeed. And great stones catapulted at the fortress walls tore gaping holes, through which even more of the icy winter winds could blow. Food supplies began to dwindle, and the people went long spells with none at all. Yet as if by superhuman powers the brotherhood would not fall, and the relentless siege continued, though the soldiers below were not without amazement. How could these ragged heretics keep enduring such attacks and travail?

But the Cathars held deep faith, and their invincible strength came from this spiritual fortitude. They could fast, they could pray, and they could endure. In their hearts they kept their unshakeable connection to their Source. And ever more fervently did they pray and offer worship to their Sun and to the Cosmic Mother-Father Creator. And their communions with worlds unseen only grew stronger as the harshness of this outer world increased. Deep within, they found refuge in the innermost sanctuary of the Heart, where no raging fires of human insanity could touch.

And Lumiere, cloistered yet deeply in the womb of the mountain, held the spiritual threads of light for her people as she always had, immersing deeper and deeper into the silence and communion with the One. This was no unfamiliar task for her. She remembered long ago… in another time, in another land, just behind the dim mists of memory…

And so she began to prepare for what was to come. They would undergo the Solar Initiations, to open the pathways back through the Sun, to the Sun beyond the Sun. They would be returning Home. Ah, Home…

where was this evasive place, this longed-for abode of
their souls?

Before springtime could awaken the promise of
rebirth and new life in the land, the end time came
for the Cathars. In early March of that dark agonizing
winter, the worn and weary Brotherhood surrendered.
They were offered their lives to be spared if they would
forsake their heretical ways and convert to the Church
doctrine. But they would rather die than forsake their
truth and allow the Light to be distorted.

And so it was the end…and on that fateful grey
day of winter's end, the last of the Cathars, the Pure
Ones, came arm and arm down the mountainside of
Montsegur. They were two hundred in number, the last
of their people. And into the fires of the Inquisition they
surrendered their earthly forms to be consumed. From
fire unto fire, their forms, like incense, were offered up
to the flames, and the spiritual fragrance of their eternal
essence returned to the great Fire of the Sun beyond the
Sun and back into formlessness.

What became of the White Rose, the Pure One,
Lumiere? Was she also consumed in these raging fires?
Or did she, in her subtle body of pure light, depart this
world even before she could be found? It is not known
for sure…but one might wonder…for can the pure light
ever truly be destroyed? Some say there were a few who
escaped Montsegur before the end, somehow secretly
departing over the back wall and down the steep cliffs at
the hidden side of the fortress. And it is whispered that
they had escaped with a treasure…

Some say it was the Holy Grail, some say it was a chest of jewels and gold; perhaps it was a golden one who was herself a Grail, a jewel and a treasure of purest golden Light…

Chapter 4
Beyond All Time

How many nights will my heart go searching for you?
When the moon is wide and white,
spilling milky light
upon the darkness...
or the deep night is unfathomably black
I have searched the starlit blackness for you...
How many times will I return,
how many lives and worlds
will call me here again,
just to find you...?

Chapter 5
Lemuria

It is said that long, long ago, hidden in the mists of time and memory, a great land and civilization once filled the Pacific seas. Lemuria, the land of Mu, the Motherland, lives in the secret dreams of those who hold a dim memory of a time when the Earth was a garden of exquisitely pure primordial beauty and harmony.

It was indeed the Motherland, the land of the Great Mother, the Source of All, whose people revered and worshipped Her in all Her ways. Since the beginning of time, since before this world was, the knowledge of Her was what had always guided them. She was the Creator, the Sustainer, the bringer of Life…She was the One who had birthed this all into Being, and who, in Her Infinite Love, nurtured and sustained all Her creation. It was She, who in union with the Father, the Sun beyond the Sun, had conceived all form in the womb of Her boundless space. How then could the people not worship and adore Her?

She was the Earth beneath their feet, who gave them Her body from which to be nourished. She it was who had woven these bodies of Her sacred elements in such perfect alchemy: earth, air, fire, water…all the mysterious forces of creation.

These bodies, all bodies, every life-form crafted with such tender care and precision, each designed with an unfathomably brilliant intelligence, all breathed into with Her sacred breath of Life.

Thus the Goddess was alive and well in the ancient

Motherland. And so the Circle of Life was intact. The people worshipped with every breath She who had given them Life, and She who sustains this life with every breath. And in turn, the giver of Life gave more and more of All that She had: all the blessed life, beauty, abundance, goodness, and health; all that She had created from Her Infinite Love. This was Her intention in Her Creation, this was Her design.

And all that was needed to continue in the perfection of this design was remembered by the people, in their days of gratitude and worship of Her. Love begets love, and so the simple truth is that as the Creator created all in Love, so does love and gratitude given back to Her by Her creation continue the circle, that it ever is complete and whole.

Tragically, there would come a time when the circle would be broken, but that sad tale will be told later, and perhaps in its telling it may serve to reawaken a long-forgotten truth. Only then, when this truth is remembered, can the possibility of genuine happiness be found again in this world. Until that time, the children of Earth struggle beneath the veils of forgetfulness that cloud their knowing of the Truth of existence. And thus do they suffer even to this day with the pangs of separation.

In those days…

The Earth was warm and moist and fertile; there were trees laden with fruit of every imaginable delicacy, flavour, and hue, and exquisite flowers blossomed profusely amidst great vast forests, jungles, and valleys of sublime beauty. Myriad in design were the lifeforms found here, all expressions of a perfect creation.

Beneath the verdant, cool canopy of the trees, the jungle floors were carpeted with a soft, green velvet moss, which to the bare feet of the people was deliciously welcoming. For indeed, the people of this land wore no shoes, nor many clothes, as they delighted in the moist, warmly enveloping air, the golden caress of sunlight upon their skin, and the soft nourishing communion with the Earth through their bare feet.

Time passed slowly here, or not at all, for the vibration of the Earth was higher then and had not yet fallen into the lower realms of mind where time exists. Theirs was a consciousness yet unified in Oneness with Source, and the people lived in a timeless awareness of Eternal Presence. Thus, what would be thousands of years if it were now measured in time, were the lengths of their lives.

Time did not imprison them, nor all the ailments it begets, neither aging nor decay nor death. A soul could consciously choose to leave their form whenever they wished, by laying their earthen body down and moving in spirit form on to higher spheres. This might happen after countless millennia, and was officiated through initiation rites presided over by the High Priestesses and Priests of the Temple of the Sun. For back through the portal of the Sun a departing spirit would journey, returning to the Source, the vast Ocean of Light, from whence they'd come.

The Temple of the Sun was golden and luminous, as it shone in the dazzling sunlight there upon the highest hilltop. Overlooking the terraced gardens that spread out down the slopes to the valley, the village and jungles below, it was magnificent to all who beheld its golden beauty. Here, in the various temples of which it was comprised, the Priestesses and Priests of the Sun held the pure Light in vigil and sacred communion with the Source. Through sacred rituals, chants, and devotions they worshipped the Mother Goddess and the Father Sun. And in this way the balance and harmony was held, the circle was kept sacred and whole, and the life of all was nourished and fulfilled. Thus the people knew only great joy and abundance beyond measure, and all was well, as it was meant to be from the beginning.

In this primordial garden there lived…

A Priestess of the temple. In truth she was High Priestess, for she bore the star symbols of Sirius upon her brow as one who held the original star codes. It was her lineage and her people who had first come at the beginning to seed this planet with the higher codes of Light from the Blue Star. They were known as Sun Gods, for they came from the Sun and from Suns beyond Suns, back to the Sun of Sirius. The Light they bore was of such golden radiance that they themselves shone as suns.

She was called Lumiere Amurai, the soft luminous one, and this she was…an embodiment of the Goddess of beauty and purity.

He was a High Priest of the lineage, a Sun God, and even as the shining Sun, so was he golden in his radiance. And thus he was known as Golden.

They had come together to this world in the very beginning. First, in their Light Bodies as drops of sunlight that dance as diamonds upon the seas, they had come. And then again they came when the lands began to coalesce and lifeforms emerged from the primordial seas, and they clothed themselves in the robes of form.

They were One, but as two they appeared, in the way of all things in this world. The One became two, male and female, to dance in the delight of polarity, and then to return again unto One.

So they were two, yet they were ever and always One, and the experience of being one, and yet two, was exquisitely exhilarating, for their consciousness had not yet fallen, as it later would, into the perception of separation, and the immense pain which that would bring. Their experience of being two was joyful and playful, as they revelled in the sweet interplay of being in two bodies, male and female.

And so they did, for long ages of timeless time, live in this unified consciousness. And if time were measured as it is now, you would say they were thousands of years in age, and yet they appeared as ageless; shining and beautiful with the radiance of the stars and the sun. Their long, flowing hair was as fine spun gold and their skin luminous with a golden light that shone from within. Their eyes were exceptionally large and shining, like great portals through which could be glimpsed the entire cosmos. His were a brilliant blue, like their Star, and hers were dark liquid pools, like the depths of space, in which the secrets of eternity were held.

They embodied the highest dimensional vibrations of Light, emanating a golden luminosity and guiding the people in the ways of the Great Mother's Infinite Love. They ensured that the delicate web of life was honoured and kept intact, teaching the ways of the Heart and reverence for all life.

It was indeed a golden age, as the golden Light of the Sun Gods shone throughout the lands.

He loved and served the Goddess through her, as the embodiment of the Divine Feminine, and his love brought her deeper into form and kept her in balance. Her love fanned the embers of his light, and the Supreme Light was assured and grew brighter, to embody the Sun within this physical dimension; a Sun God in all his majesty. The alchemy of their union generated grace and blessings throughout the lands.

She spoke the Light Language of the stars, chanting prayers and praise to the Great Mother Goddess and the Father Sun, prayers that echoed throughout the valleys as celestial harmonies, keeping the vibrations high, clear, and pure. He guided the people in the righteous ways of Nature, the tending of the Earth and the alchemies of herbs, plants, and precious stones. And they served all the people in remembering the sacred ways, the ways of reverence and respect for all life and the Source of all life.

Long were the days the Sun Gods dwelt amongst the people and long the age when golden Love reigned. It seemed it would never end.

Ah, but alas, it did…

<hr>

It was in early springtime, when the moon was waxing to her fullest light, that there was held a great celebration for the season of rebirth and the return of the Solar Deity to His high throne in the heavens. And though there was never truly winter in those days, there were subtle changes of season as Mother Earth danced ever so lightly about Father Sun.

And the people danced as well, and glorious music was made that sounded across the mountains and valleys, and was echoed by the chorus of millions of birds singing from the vast forests, singing in exultation of life. A great feast was prepared for the celebration, a feast of every luscious fruit that ripened under the Sun, all dripping with the golden nectar of life-giving Love.

Was not the joy and exaltation of life the greatest form of worship? For the Great Cosmic Mother delighted in Her children's joy and had created them all to live in unending ecstasy and bliss.

The darkness of pain and separation had never yet shadowed their innocent hearts; they knew only the bliss of being one with all in perfect Love.

But this, alas, was about to change. For in this auspicious time of rebirth, when all were in joyous celebration, something else was felt amidst the Priests and Priestesses of the Temple. As the people of the land danced and feasted in reverent celebration of life, high above in the Temple of the Sun a Council was called amidst the Priesthood. They needed to speak of what had been perceived in the subtle currents: an unrest that had been brewing for some time.

Far away across the planet, on another great continent of a distant sea, there existed another civilization: the ancient and mighty land of Atlantis, which had also been begotten of the light, having been seeded as well long ago by star beings of a higher consciousness.

In the beginning the light was pure and shining in this land, as were the beings who had seeded it from distant star systems. But in later times there came to be there representatives of more than a few star nations, and not all of them were in resonance with the Heart. So it was that this began to erode the very foundations of the civilization, and what emerged from the once pure and fair Atlantis was something distorted and dissonant with the natural order of existence.

Slowly, insidiously, the distortion seeped into the fabric of Atlantean culture, and the people began to forget their origin in the Light and their union with the Heart of the Great Mother.

The sacred rituals were forgotten; the worship of Source, that kept them in alignment, was disappearing. Deemed now as insignificant and even childish, they began to worship instead their own power of intellect. This schism with the Heart was disastrous, and the dissonance created began to ripple through all the layers of the culture.

The intellect was revered and the false power that it gave became an intoxicant. The people began to assume themselves sovereign in their creations and became enthralled with their own minds as they developed more and more complex technologies, technologies that had increasingly less and less regard for the Earth and for life and the subtle essences of Heart that create and sustain it.

The Mind, when not in union with Heart, becomes tyrannical and destructive, for the holy balance of masculine and feminine principle is lost. Thus it began to be in the great and mighty land of Atlantis, and the shadows of separation created by this split began to darken the minds and hearts of the people.

They no longer worshipped the One Source, through

the Cosmic Mother and the Father Sun, but began to worship instead their own minds and all the distorted creations thereof. They assumed a power they were not in balance enough to wield, for Love, the only true power, now no longer guided their course. They put their reliance on technologies outside of themselves, forgetting the true powers, the inner divine technologies that lay within. And their creations, the technologies, that once were intended for the benefit of the people, began to reflect instead the destructiveness and darkness of their own minds as they fell deeper and deeper into separation.

No longer did they regard life as sacred, but instead they saw it as something to be manipulated and controlled. Their thirst for power grew as their creations grew more complex and destructive. It seemed incomprehensible, but the Sun, the Sacred One, was forgotten, even loathed, as they imagined themselves more powerful even than their Source.

This darkness grew, like a festering virus, in the hidden recesses of their separated and troubled minds, and the Pure Light that had once shone so brilliantly upon the crystalline shores of mighty Atlantis could no more be found.

Then the unthinkable happened...they developed technologies so dissonant with the natural and holy order of existence that life indeed could not endure.

———

But far away, across the distant seas, in the Motherland, the whispers of foreboding were felt. For the Earth is One, and what happens in one part cannot be separated from any other part. All that happens here must affect there, and all that occurs there does indeed affect here. One sacred web of life connects all, and if it is broken in any place, the whole web is damaged.

The Priestesses and Priests of Mu had long sensed the rising darkness that was across the planet. They could feel it in their bodies and in their hearts, they could sense it in the air, and it came upon the easterly winds like a shadowy whisper of foreboding. High in the towers of the Temples, they watched the signs in the stars and they knew...

And so a Council was held, and those who could read the stars told what they saw, and those who could hear the whispers in the wind whispered what they heard, and those who listened in the silence of their own hearts only sat in stillness, and glistening tears fell softly down their cheeks from their closed eyes.

It was not that fear shadowed their minds, for fear had never been known to them, being as they were in the highest vibrations of Love. And they understood that in the vast scheme of all that is, Love alone shall and does prevail. But even as the day gives way to the night, so they could sense that a night was coming, and a dark shadow would cover the sun...for a time.

And so it was in the land of Mu, that garden of inexpressible delight, that a certain sadness was felt for the very first time. The Priestesses and Priests of the Sun convened in Council for many days, and prayers were offered and sacred rituals made, and the High Priestess Lumiere chanted the star songs of Sirius, to come into clearer resonance with the High Councils of the Sun.

Why was this darkness occurring? And what was to be done...? The answer came thus...

"Far amidst the shining stars,
your heart of Light does rest...
In pure Love all forms are born, to magnify the One.
Within the Heart of the All are vast universes turning...
Within the depths of human hearts
a ceaseless, tender yearning
reaches up to touch the stars, to touch and melt
and merge in Light...
toward a radiant sun, the Eternal One,
shining beyond the night.
Close your eyes in gentleness,
to the stillness once more find your way...
Breathe a breath of gentle peace
and let all the world fall away...
The stars are calling you Home,
to the starry heavens within.
The angels are calling you Home
to the One you have always been...
As Source, the One, the All
remember from whence you come,
from One vast Heart of Infinite Love
your Light comes into form...
And surely it is but a dreaming
that ever you could be apart...
There is but One who Is,
One Self, One Soul, One Heart..."

And those present in the Council listened, and turned deeply within to the stillness, allowing the words to awaken their knowings, and the world to fall away, as the High Priestess Lumiere had sung her song.

Then they remembered this world as a Dream dreamed by the Dreamer of All, and they knew that beyond all that appears, there is only that One who is Infinite Love; all else is illusion. And their hearts were comforted in this remembrance.

When they had sat thus in this silence of communion for a long while, then at last one spoke…and it was the High Priest himself, Golden, and his words came forth as rays of light, speaking with authority, and as one in the masculine form.

"Even as we rest in the eternal embrace of Absolute Being and know all is well, so also here in this world are we moved by immutable forces, that as tides of the sea would carry us out like the sacred Breath of life. And so there is that within us that moves us as certain as the tides and the breath, to respond and take action. Yet though it may be all but a dream, still within this dream are we also moved by compassion and need, when dangers arise. Thus, is it not deemed so, that we respond to this that we feel as a danger? Shall we not go forth across the seas, to do what we can to abate this darkness that arises?"

And amongst the Priests there came a certain sigh of acknowledgement and a subtle nod of heads. And Lumiere heard her beloved and knew the truth in his words. What was destined to be, would be. There would be action taken.

Thus it was determined that a small band of the wisest and bravest of the priests of the Temple of the Sun would go forth with Golden to the distant shores of Atlantis. Here they would seek Council with the Atlantean elders and see what peace and healing intervention they might bring to that troubled land.

With haste the preparations were made; they must go with the fullness of the springtime moon, the auspicious time of new beginnings. And so the ships were readied, and it was to be that upon the second eve of the springtime celebrations, when the moon was at her fullest, they set sail.

While in the village all the people were feasting and rejoicing, Lumiere climbed alone to the rise of the highest hill above the sea. Here she could watch the ships depart. Silent, her heart heavy with unspeakable feelings, she watched the fateful departure. The full moon had risen and was casting a luminous ribbon of light upon the sea, and it was upon this silvery pathway of light that the ships glided, their great silken sails billowing out behind them.

From the valley below, the melodic strains of music from the village wafted out across the waters, accentuating the poignancy of their departure. A light, flower-scented breeze softly caressed her bare arms, and she shivered. She saw the sails catch that same sweet breeze, and they rippled softly and waved a silken response, as if in farewell.

Lumiere was silent for a long time, as she watched the ships move farther out to sea. Her eyes were wide and luminous in the moonlight; only now, at last, as the ships disappeared over the horizon of the sea, could she allow her tears to flow.

Many cycles of the moon passed, as she watched with her inner vision their journeys across the seas and their landing upon the distant shores of Atlantis. She vigilantly held the Light for all that would transpire, keeping the inner planes clear of interference for the brave emissaries. But there was much that she saw that made her heart ache.

Beneath many starry nights and many sunlit days, she waited and watched and often wept. She saw…and she knew…more than she ever wanted to see or know. And she missed her beloved Golden so deeply, even though they were never not in inner heart communion.

She missed his beautiful form beside her, his great shining eyes, and his knowing smile. She missed his laughter, his warm embrace, and his tender loving touch. She missed his fragrant hair that would spill across her face as they lay together at night. Yes, she missed him, although yet they remained inseparable on the inner planes and she could hear him clearly as he told her all that was transpiring.

Her only consolation was to go deeper into the silence to commune with the Solar Councils for guidance… and to listen to the ever-present heartbeat of the Great Mother. She understood that the outcome of this journey would be a turning point for all; a great shift would indeed happen. And she must stay unwavering in her alignment to Source, to hold the Light no matter what.

In the golden light of the mornings she would walk amongst the people, radiating love and comfort and strength to all, as their spiritual leader, never belying the quivering that was in her heart. And as the warmth of the day waxed strong, she liked to go alone into the cool forest and lie beneath the spreading verdant canopy.

Upon the forest floor, carpeted with soft velvet green

moss, she would lie. The feeling upon her bare skin was cool and moist and ever so comforting. High above in the trees, myriad colourful birds flitted and offered her their melodious songs of joy. And often in the spreading branches above her, great sphinx moths hung suspended, their giant wings, the length of a man, were spread out, displaying exquisitely intricate patterns in delicate shades of silvery grey and golden brown. Sometimes, when standing, she could reach up and stroke the soft velvety length of their giant bodies. They would quiver with her touch and flutter ever so lightly their great patterned wings. This would always make her laugh with delight. And so it was that in these rare and precious moments she forgot her cares for a time.

Often on these walks she was accompanied by her beloved companion, Ramu, who was a great silver grey panther. He walked beside her, gliding silently on his big padded paws, across the green mossy forest floor, leaning sometimes against her leg to be stroked. Ramu would lie beside her and they would fall into a deep, restful sleep, cradled in the nurturing verdant embrace of the forest. It was one of these times, when they were lying such, that Lumiere had a dream…

She saw the beautiful face of her beloved Golden, his piercingly blue eyes gazing deep into hers. Then she could see that his look was one of intense anguish. She felt his heart, his sorrow and longing for her, and slowly his beautiful eyes began to glisten with tears.

Then she understood. She needed no words; their hearts were one. She awoke with a start, her heart beating wildly, her breath shallow and quick. And knowing she would not see her beloved again in this life, she began to sob.

The Atlanteans would have nothing to do with the priestly emissaries from Lemuria. They looked upon them as inferior heathens, whom they disdained. Unyielding in their stance of power, they disregarded any council of the Heart and the Way of the Great Mother as weak and foolish. The Atlanteans worshipped power, but they had forgotten the true power, the only power, which is Love.

For the cycles of two moons, Golden and his Priests stayed amongst the Atlantean culture, doing what they could to appeal to the hearts of the people. There were a few who recognized the truth they offered, for deep within them lived a dim memory of their luminous origins and a time long ago when Atlantis was pure and untainted.

Those that could be awakened, Golden awakened, and as he sensed with his inner knowing that time was short, he gathered those few to him to prepare for an exodus. The Solar Councils of Sirius were telepathically relaying messages to him, directing him to make haste with readying the boats for departure. He was told they must sail not the way they had come, but in the opposite direction, to the east. This was an unknown sea, and it meant journeying farther from their Homeland. The way Home was not safe, he was given to understand. The approaching cataclysm that was imminent would render that direction impossible to navigate.

He was shown no more of where they were to go, other than to the east, but the urgency of timing was clear…they were to depart quietly and secretly in the dark, moonless hours of that very night.

The Priestess seeresses of the Golden Temple of Mu saw the destruction coming, long before the first great wave hit the peaceful shores of the Motherland. They had for some time felt the undercurrents in the ethers and read the troubled signs in the stars. They had felt the whisperings of pain coming upon the subtlest winds and glanced the first shadows covering the Sun.

As High Priestess, Lumiere guided her Priestesses in ritual preparations for the Solar Initiations of opening the pathways back through the Sun. They were not afraid of death, for in truth they had never known death. It did not exist, for they knew themselves as one with Eternal Being. It was instead a conscious departing of the body, to return back through the doorway of the Sun, back Home to Source.

She gathered the people of the land and instructed them to go deeply within and draw near to the Great Mother and find refuge in Her Heart, from which they had been created and back to which they would return. Thus the people were prepared to make the shift consciously from form to formlessness, to return in waves of Light back into the Heart of the Sun.

When she felt she had done all that she could, she left her Priestesses to stay with the people, and she made her way back to the Temple. There was no more she could do now, but to hold unwaveringly the flame of Light that would guide the souls back through the Solar Portal.

Thus she went alone, as the dusky twilight began to descend, to the high altar room of the Golden Temple of the Sun. Here she was to keep vigil through that long, moonless night, holding the Light anchored deep into this dimension as the solar pathways opened. By dawn and the rising of the Sun, it would be done.

She remembers it well…even now after aeons of time have passed and other lives and lands and people have come and gone. She remembers it well, as if it were but yesterday, when the Great Wave hit the balmy shores of Mu, and the Earth shook and trembled and groaned and cracked. She remembers it well, the silent agony…as alone in the Temple of the Sun, she felt the shuddering blow, and in deepest communion with the One, gathered all her energy into her innermost heart. Then with one last long, deep breath, she left her body and returned unto the Light.

Chapter 6
Between the Worlds

The Light was blinding...she spun in a dizzying spiral toward the Sun, and the brilliant luminosity of ten thousand suns...

She had journeyed through the heart of the Sun before ~ many times ~ during her long incarnation in Lemuria. The Priests and Priestesses of Mu were Sun Gods ~ they knew the way well. But always they had remained connected to their form bodies by an etheric silver cord. This allowed them to return after sojourns through the solar portal back to Sirius.

Our Sun and all suns are indeed interdimensional doorways, wormholes, so to speak, that connect all the suns of the galaxy back to the Central Sun. When summoned, here they could pass through the myriad suns and solar councils, to the Council of the Christ, in the heart of the Sirian Sun. But always they would return, following the silver cord back to their form bodies in Mu.

This time was different, very different. Her silver cord was loosed and severed from her earthen body, and hence there would be no going back. It was over. This life, this precious embodiment in Lemuria, and indeed Lemuria itself, was a chapter now closed.

They had not known death in the Motherland ~ only circles within circles of Being, wherein there was no beginning and no end. And in the highest truth of existence, there cannot be. For Being is eternal. Being is birthless and deathless, and only that which appears to be born can appear to die. Before and beyond all appearances of birth and death and endings is That which is changeless and eternal. And it was this knowing in which they had abided and lived, such that the very cells of their bodies were inhabited by the consciousness of Eternal Being. This was the secret of their long lives... the complete identification with the Eternal timeless essence of Being, rather than the ephemeral forms subject to the changing tides of Time. Thus, they were masters of Time, rather than its subjects.

But the intensity of the Light now was such as she had not known before... and she utterly dissolved into it until nothing remained. Or so it seemed...

The dissolution of her form body was like the shattering of a billion shards of crystal flung across the universe. If she could have described the experience, which of course she could not, she would have said that it felt like the end.

It would be long ages before Lumiere would again take embodiment on Earth. Living through those last days...the last days of her beloved Mu, was more than she could bear. And the separation from Golden...that was a ripping apart of the very fabric of her soul. Her delicate essence was shattered, like so many pieces of a crystal, that once broken can never be put together again as it was.

From the Councils of the Sun it was determined that she must be sent to the healing temples of Venus, once more, where the rarefied atmosphere of purest love could begin to mend the shattered fibres of her being. She would need to be recalibrated to adjust to the higher vibrational frequencies of this luminous dimensional realm, of course, but once that was adjusted, she would surely heal in these powerful fields of love and beauty. She returned to Venus and the Light Temples there to heal her fractured soul.

Meanwhile on Earth, Golden had followed the guidance of the Sirian Council and set sail east from Atlantis before the great cataclysm destroyed the continent. The once fair and mighty Atlantis disappeared altogether, as the quaking and troubled Earth groaned with agony, brought about by the terrible misuse of energies that had afflicted her, and with one mighty explosion sank beneath the angry sea.

The Earth would tremble with such force that the massive waves, after swallowing Atlantis, would continue to ripple and rage and swell far across the western sea, and at last arrive at the innocent shores of Mu.

And thus it was that the Great Fall came upon the Earth. The golden age of the Pure Shining Ones would come to an end, as the frequency of the planet would spiral down into denser and denser vibrations. So dense, that over the long ages of the Fall, almost all remembrance of these luminous lands would be forgotten.

Are all our dreams and visions lost?
Scattered upon the cold, cruel winds of fate…
and dimmed our pure, true knowing
of our hearts' clear light…

Where have you gone, my love,
when now falls the deepest night?
When all the paths are shadowed 'neath the darkness
of a starless sky
where do we find refuge now
when our hearts want only to cry…?

A dark abyss of emptiness now lies between our hearts
since that night the north wind blew
and tore us far apart…

And will you not remember me
as the rose you once loved well
whose golden heart you watered
lest her petals fell…

Chapter 7
Venus

On the higher dimensions of Venus, there exists a whole civilization of such luminosity and beauty as to have no parallel upon the Earth plane. There is a great city of Light, which is comprised solely of temples which appear to be made entirely of transparent, shimmering crystal.

Each temple is dedicated to the highest qualities of Divine Love and Beauty, for this is the essence of Venusian atmosphere; the very air is Love, a love that permeates everything, and the natural expression of it is sublime beauty. As the frequency of this higher dimension of Venus is too high to support duality, consciousness is completely unified in the One, and that One is Infinite Love.

In the centre and heart of the city, there stands, like a great shining jewel, the magnificent Temple of the Kumaras, where High Council is held. These great and beneficent beings are the lineage of planetary guardians who oversee with great care the destiny for planet Earth.

Through their immense love and overlighting presence, the Earth has been guided through her difficult evolutionary processes as gently as possible. If not for their compassionate interventions, the Earth and all life upon her would have long since vanished. Not unlike a loving parent, who must watch over a child so patiently and unconditionally, allowing him to experience the necessary growing pains as he makes his way toward maturity, so the lineage of Kumaras have for long ages held the light for Earth's unfolding destiny.

All life in the cosmos is in an ever-expanding evolutionary process, and cosmic law provides that those who evolve to higher levels must turn and assist those who are yet behind them. The planet Venus had attained her ascension long ago and was blessed to now be in a vibrational dimension that was free of the suffering of the lower dimensions that are yet in duality. Thus, with great compassion, the Venusians were committed to assisting the Earth with her ascension. They held the vision and the knowing that one day Earth, too, would be a luminous, shining Love Star, inhabited by awakened conscious beings. And to this end, they held the divine blueprint unwaveringly.

Before coming to Earth, the Sun Gods of Sirius first were sent to Venus to be prepared. Here they could step down their frequency from the formless light of Sirius and coalesce bodies of form. Luminous form, albeit unseen to the eyes of Earth, until it was stepped down once more into the bodies of the Physical dimension.

Thus it was, that both Lumiere and Golden had first been prepared on Venus before they had come to Earth. And in Lemuria, their bodies were still vibrating quite high, for the Earth had not yet fallen and could still support their frequency. So indeed, they were yet luminous in their golden beauty. But if one of Earth were to behold them on Venus…well, you would not see them at all, for they would appear invisible to eyes not of that dimensional frequency.

The cataclysm of Atlantis was a disastrous setback for Earth's evolution, to say the least. There had been so much potential unfolding there, with the presence of the Sirian Sun Gods in the Motherland. And it had seemed that the divine plan for the planet's ascension was proceeding beautifully.

Ah, but this was a universe of free will, a necessary attribute for the development of consciousness. By free will alone must beings choose to create their destiny. And even as a child who might be inclined by curiosity to play with fire and then puts his hand in the flame many times before he finally realizes that it burns, so the children of Earth might also have to learn from creating painful experiences. Maybe they would also have to do it over and over again before they would finally learn to make a different choice? Ah, but time was not an issue, for it did not even exist to the Sirians, and so if aeons of evolution are destroyed on Earth, it would just have to start again. They would not give up. Nor would the Venusians, who were working in resonance with Sirius.

The Star-seeding of the Earth by the Sirians was a grand experiment. Could they introduce this higher dimensional consciousness into a realm that was vibrating yet so slowly? Could it then germinate in the womb of time, that strange phenomena unknown in the higher dimensions, and eventually bear the fruit of a new Earth and a new species of beings who would at once be embodied in physical matter, yet be awake in divine higher consciousness? A cross, so to speak…materialized spirit and spiritualized matter.

This possibility had captivated them for aeons of timeless time; it held so much potential. For on Sirius form did not exist, it was all light; and the Earth, this beautiful blue planet positioned just so from her Sun, was a perfect cradle for physical materialized form.

To imagine the implications…materialized embodied Gods!

Within the Council chambers of Venus, at the very centre, is the sacred Three-Fold Flame, which burns undying throughout the ages, emanating the three divine qualities of Love, Wisdom, and Power. Hence it is three colours: rose pink, which represents Divine Love; crystalline blue, for Divine Wisdom; and golden yellow, which is Divine Power. Together these qualities comprise perfected consciousness.

Each of the temples throughout the city has the function of holding the vibrations of one of these three qualities, and hence is represented in one of these flames that burn within the Temple of the Kumaras. It is a beautiful three-fold flame, ever burning in luminous rose, sapphire, and golden light.

Before her descent to Earth, Lumiere had been the Priestess for the Temple of Love's Purity, which is the vibrational emanation that shines through each of the three flames when they are unified in their highest expression. Her essence was of such a refined nature of purity that simply her presence was enough to amplify that quality and emanate it back through the Three-Fold Flame, where it would continue to bless and keep the energies for the whole planet in harmony. Had it not always been so? It was her design from the beginning, when coming in her formless light-body from the Sun of Sirius, she first stepped down her vibration enough to appear in even the lightest Venusian form.

Here on Venus the forms were indeed luminous, nearly transparent, and unspeakably beautiful. Those souls who are chosen to follow the star paths from the very high vibrations of Sirius to the lower planes of Earth must first pass through Venus to be prepared. They are assisted in stepping down their frequency to make it possible to enter the denser realms of Earth. But many there are who choose not to continue the arduous descent to Earth from Venus, it being extremely difficult to lower their frequency sufficiently. These then remain in the rarefied Venusian atmosphere, to serve the Earth from afar.

Thus Lumiere remained in the timeless dimensions of Venus long after the fall of Lemuria and held for the Earth the divine vibrations of Love's Pure Light as the frequency of the planet continued to spiral down lower and lower and consciousness densified under matter's spell.

She held that pure vibration of Love for her beloved Golden, whose destiny it was to fall with the Earth through myriad lifetimes. This was the mandate from the Councils, for the seed of Light must not be lost; it must be planted deeper now, in the darkness that would envelop the fallen planet.

Being the other part of his soul, she would be able to hold the cords of light that would keep him connected, even if only by a slender thread of memory, as he made the treacherous descent into the lower frequencies of the falling planet.

He would forget, oh, yes, he would…but she would always be holding the threads of remembrance for him. And the time would come, long ages hence, when he would remember once more. There would come a time when the Light Codes of Earth would be reawakened.

And they would meet again.

How many nights will my heart go searching for you?
When the moon is wide and white
spilling milky light
across the sky…
or when the night has no moon, yet is ablaze with light
I've called you from afar,
through the silence of our Star,
to find you in the secret depths of my heart's aching.
How many times will I return,
how many lives and worlds
will call me here again,
to find you…?

Chapter 8
Golden

Golden fought to withhold his tears as he and his men made their way across the strange and tumultuous seas. He could not let his guard down now, not enough to allow himself to feel the overwhelming agony of what was transpiring. They had set sail two days before the great cataclysm of Atlantis, and now in the distance, on the far western horizon, the sky glowed an eerie orange hue with the telling of the fiery explosion that had taken the continent down.

He knew his homeland was also gone, that his beloved Lumiere was gone, all that he loved was gone… but he dare not feel. He had to stay strong now and guide his ships across the ravaging seas…to where, he knew not.

His heart was numb, like a hard, cold stone. The tears choked back, his great blue eyes staring straight ahead. Somehow the endless hours passed, the days wore on, a blur of grey waves and grey sullen skies, dark starless nights, and black churning waters. He did not sleep, he did not eat, he did not speak. His mind was numb, in shock, too stunned to think.

Somewhere inside he knew everything, but he could not touch his knowing. It was hot and painful, and he pulled away from its burn. He had no choice but to bury this inconceivable grief deep in the recesses of his being.

Time passed…was it days or weeks or months? No one could say. But one grey morning, just after dawn, they sighted the first land.

They had never known grief or pain or separation in Lemuria. These feelings were all completely unknown to them. But the frequency was falling fast now, and these feelings were in accord with the lowering vibrations. In the unified consciousness of Love, the Lemurians had always lived. Golden did not even know how to feel these strange and foreign feelings. It was like suddenly having to breathe air after being a creature of the sea, and with this first breath of something so foreign, the air burned and was bitter to the taste.

So it happened that in his soul, there was a fragmenting that occurred. In order to withstand the pressure of the denser frequency he now was entering, part of him split off and disappeared. It separated into a shadowland of unconsciousness, and here these painful feelings remained.

For lifetimes hence, he would be shadowed by these feelings that lay deeply buried within. Only in the fullness of time might they ripen and surface, to finally be felt and released. Only then, and who knows when that would be, could his heart truly be whole again.

So this was the beginning of forgetting...and it was to be the pattern for the lower dimensional experience. A fragmentation from feeling and knowing, and hence from being one's self fully. This would be the experience of all upon the Earth in the times to come.

Why did it have to be this way? Why was Golden not allowed to return to Venus with Lumiere and be healed in the Light Temples there? Ah, but the greater design of our destinies is mysterious. Our fair, noble Golden was to venture deep into the densities over many lifetimes upon Earth, to be an emissary of Light going down into the fabric of the darkness. And like a lifeline, would keep the connection to Source, even if only partially consciously, established in the darkest depths, until a pre-ordained time when the codes were once more awakened in his fibres, signalling the time of completion.

Then the Light Codes could ripple all the way into the densest depths of the Earth through him, for the pathway had to be made by his willingness to go to those depths. This was in his design, and the courage and sacrifice it required defies imagination.

Even Golden himself had little understanding of how dark it would be. How could he? He had never before known anything but the unified consciousness of Infinite Love and the luminosity of its full expression.

Far away, on another world, in dimensional distances that cannot be measured, Lumiere would be holding the other end of the golden light, the thread that would be his lifeline. He would not be able to commune with her, nor to leave his body as once he could, to travel back to Venus. Nor would he, for the most part, even remember his connection there, except perhaps in his dreams. But she would be holding the thread...

He would still have the ability to travel out of his body into the Astral Planes around Earth, in his sleeping state, but not beyond. And this access would allow him some relief from the otherwise overwhelming density of the fallen planet.

Aeons would pass...and for Golden, to whom time had never existed, time now would be his reality. Alas, time would be his prison, but also it was to be the force he must work either with or against to forge the pathways Home.

They came ashore on a land so distinct from where they had come. Gone were the lush forests and jungles of home, and in their place were golden sands, devoid of all vegetation. The landscape spread far before them, open and empty of life…and the Sun beat down mercilessly hot on this desolate golden desert. Gone were the verdant green forests that had offered them everything: shade, food, shelter, the melodic songs of birds, and a restful green to the eyes. Here it was startlingly bright; hot golden sun reflecting on hot golden sands, far to the distant horizons, and so silent, as it seemed no life stirred here.

It was decided that they would board the ships once again and sail along the coast of this strange and desolate land, to see if some sign of life might be found. So this they did, and after some time, some sparse vegetation was sighted along the rocky coastline. Then trees began to appear, tall palms that waved gracefully in the breezes, and shorter shrubs beneath. Soon after, there appeared to be a settlement of some sort, with scattered structures built of stone and clay and palm fronds. Here they chose to once more come to shore.

The people of this strange land were welcoming; they came to greet the boats with great curiosity. They were dark-skinned and they smiled easily, setting the wayfarers at ease. The language they spoke was not known, but with time this seemed to pose no problem, as they expressed much with their eyes and hands and had a very open, childlike way about them.

Golden felt his heart touched by the innocent, trusting quality of these simple people, and for the first time in a very long while he began to feel he could relax a bit. They would be safe here. Safe? What a strange concept…Golden was perplexed by this feeling, for in Lemuria they had never before known fear, and thus the idea of safety was unknown. Well, at least not until those last days…

Yet this was the feeling…yes, that it was safe. Safe to rest, safe to be…

The people of this land were a good, simple people. They received the Lemurians as Gods, and indeed Sun Gods they were, although already Golden was beginning to forget what that meant. For the effects of the lowering frequencies were felt, and deep within him he knew there was something he must do before the falling consciousness would render it impossible, before he would forget everything.

Yes, they must create a way to keep the sacred wisdom of the Sun Gods from being lost altogether. They must themselves seed the Light in this land, before it was too late, and all was forgotten.

Once they had established a way of communication, Golden and his Priests began to impart to the people what they could of the Sacred Ways, of all that they had brought with them from Sirius: the worship of the Sun, as Source, and the Great Mother Goddess, whom they remembered with every prayerful breath. They imparted the healing wisdom of the Ancients and the secrets of the healing plants and herbs.

In the stones they would etch maps back to the stars,

as signs that could be left to help those who would come later to remember something of their star origins. For the veils of forgetfulness would indeed fall heavily upon the inhabitants of Earth; there must be signs, clues, symbols, monuments...

And so the works began.

In sacred geometric patterns of star-configurations and solar alignments, they constructed structures for remembrance. Facing the rising Sun at His highest throne in the summer heavens, the windows opened toward the east to align with Source at these auspicious times. These would be reminders of the pathway Home. Great stone monuments, half lion, half man, gazing toward Sirius, toward the Home Star, from which the Councils of Light would mutely speak, "Look to the stars...to your origin!"

Structures of remembrance...remembrance...

For unless it was set in stone, it would surely be forgotten, as the sands of time blew stronger and covered the land and the minds and hearts of man with dust. They would instil the pure essence of all the ancient, sacred ways, and perhaps...perhaps, some of it would withstand the Fall and carry on into the later days.

Aeons passed...

Time, illusion though it may be in the higher planes of existence, upon the Earth now was a great force that wrought change. Many lifetimes Golden had, too many to tell, each one venturing deeper into the darkness of Matter's spell.

Yes, he forgot much...who he really was, where he had come from, and why he had come at all. All that the darkness held, and all that the duality of the now fallen Earth offered, he experienced. And always, from afar, and yet a distance beyond measure, beyond time and space, in the eternal timelessness of the rarefied dimensions of Venus, Lumiere held the golden thread of Light for him. It would be long ages in Earth time, yet no more than a moment in the timelessness wherein she dwelt, before they would meet again.

⸻

There are moments in our blindness
when we know not what we have done,
and deny our hearts' knowing
as clouds obscure the sun...

Will you not remember me
before the darkness fully descends
as the one who held the Light for you,
your truest love beyond all time
your ancient and faithful friend...

⸻

Chapter 9
Yeshua

And so the long ages upon the Earth flowed on like a ceaseless river, and much changed. Yet, in the rarefied atmosphere of Venus, no time had passed. And here, in these higher dimensional frequencies of pure Love and Beauty, Lumiere experienced no sense of pain or loss from either her beloved Golden or her cherished Mu. The vibration of Venus was too high for pain to exist. She dwelt in an Eternal Now of unified consciousness, in an inexpressible bliss, beyond all sense of separation, as was now the experience upon the Earth. Here she was bathed in these exquisitely luminous vibrations, and her soul that had been so shattered upon leaving the Earth was now healed.

Like a shining jewel, she radiated the light of Love's purity throughout those luminous realms and beyond. Anyone who would gaze up from the Earth to Venus would indeed be awed by the diamond light brilliance of that beautiful star. It would ever be a shining reminder and reflection of our true divine nature, a reflection so needed by a world that had forgotten.

But soon it would come to pass…that a great change was again in the air…

<hr>

When the great Master of Love, Yeshua, began his descent from Sirius to eventually embody on Earth, he

95

came first to Venus, as all must who are making this arduous passage. Even as he had been prepared in the Councils of the Solar Christ within the Sun of Sirius, so would he also need to be prepared for his difficult Earth mission within the Temples of Venus. His destiny to be an embodiment of perfect Love, Wisdom, and Power upon the Earth at a time when the vibrational atmosphere of the planet had fallen into almost unimaginable density was no small task.

It had already been long ages since the Fall and the ensuing dimensional shift that had rendered the vibrations of Earth at the very lowest. Humans had become barbarians, having lost all sense of Oneness with Source. They no longer even remembered the Sun nor the Great Mother, Source of all life. They now regarded nothing sacred, not even life. And so they carelessly destroyed as they wished, taking without thought or remorse the lives of other creatures—animals, trees, plants, and even other humans. In their dark desperation and intense pain of separation, they raged at life, and killing and inflicting pain became some distorted way of trying to free themselves of their own unbearable suffering.

Yeshua was to embody as a man in this dark and hostile atmosphere. It was already known that his life would be brief and tumultuous, yet of utmost importance, for he would be re-seeding and anchoring a Light that the Earth had not seen in long ages. It would be a ray of hope amidst the unfathomable darkness.

So, he was to be initiated in the deepest alchemies of Love during his sojourn upon the Love Star. It was necessary for him to spend time in each of the crystalline temples of Venus to receive all the divine qualities of

Love's Pure Light. He would be required to know how to hold the purest vibrations of Love unwaveringly in the midst of the greatest challenges of darkness and pain. The Three-Fold Flame must be firmly established within his heart, so that he could draw from that reservoir of Love, Wisdom, and Power.

The Kumaras were very pleased with this high, pure, and courageous soul, and they trained him well in the attributes of compassion and selflessness. And when it came time for him to continue his journey on to Earth, a certain few of the Venusian Council were chosen to accompany him.

So it was that Lumiere was to come once again into Earth embodiment.

Some time before Yeshua made his descent to Earth, there came before him some other Sirian Star-seeded ones to prepare the way. Out of the land now known as Egypt, there arose a sect of Healers known as the Theraputai. These nomadic people were reputed for their healing abilities, and they came across the desert lands, touching and healing the people as they went. These were the earliest order of what would be known as the Essenes, the healers, the people of essence, and they came to be established in remote communities along the Dead Sea.

A mysterious people, no one knew their origin nor understood their strange ways. But true Healers they were, and indeed, healing was much needed everywhere they went. They lived simply and quietly, away from the normal society of the time, and they followed a lifestyle that was completely different from the prevailing culture.

Their primary focus was purity, in every way. Hence they wore only handspun garments of white, to represent purity; ate no flesh of animals nor food that was cooked and thus rendered impure and devoid of lifeforce; and tended the land and grew the fruits, vegetables, and herbs that sustained them. They fasted often, to maintain purity of body and mind, slept beneath the stars, and communed with the elemental forces of earth, air, fire, and water and were guided by the course of the stars.

They worshipped the Sun and all life under the Sun, revering the Solar Father as our Heavenly Father, source of our Spirit, and the Earthly Mother as source of our bodies, She who would take care of all our embodied needs. Their respect for life was integral in their healing practices, for how can one heal if one is not attuned to the very Source of all life?

To the Theraputai, women were regarded with equal respect with men, which was not so in the normal society, where women were considered inferior and segregated. These simple people, who followed such radically different lifestyles, came only to quietly establish peace and healing in a time of darkness.

The wise elders of the Order, upon communing with the stars, read the signs in the heavens, and they understood the subtlest messages foretold there. They had been divinely guided across the deserts by the Light of the One Star. The Council of Sirius transmitted guidance to them in the ancient Language of Light, and thus they knew they were to prepare the way for one who would be coming, one who carried the Codes of Light.

Thus it was that Yeshua, the chosen one, was to be born into embodiment within this order of the Essenes.

How dark it was when you arrived…
you felt it all so deeply, and it hurt.
Who could ever say how heavy was the weight upon your
wings…
Only the morning glories in the field
attested to your light…
in innocence they opened to an inner sun.
But far more fragile than these were you…
O little angel come to Earth
surely you did not know how far you had come
nor how dark it was,
nor how deep the forces.
Somewhere in that passage
you closed your eyes and fell asleep
there was so much you could not bear to see…
through the dark night of a planet you slumbered
holding in your heart a light from a distant star,
a witness of the realms from which you had come
long ago and from so very far.
Like a seed the light slept in the womb of Earth,
like a candle the tiny flame flickered in the night ~
a sacred gift from the infinite
a point of contact, a light…
and you embodied this in your heart,
even when in your silent slumber you forgot ~
in loving embrace your angelic brethren held you,
they never left you,
you never were alone.
From far beyond the starry galaxies
messages of light were sent from Home.

When first you beheld the Earth
it was from the realms of Light
and the darkness perceived, and the sorrow
your innocent heart could not bear.
In compassionate plea you cried out,
"I will go,"
though in your innocence you could not know
what that meant…
But the love so divine
that is God, that is All, that is you
you could no more bear to see unawakened
in the hearts of any of God's children
nor the Light that is All and Ever-present
be veiled from any world.
"I will go…"
And the Light penetrated the darkness,
love touched so gently a world weeping,
and you clothed yourself in Matter's embrace.
How dark it was when we arrived
how deep the forces
yet the ever-quickening Light beckons our awakening
and on the wings of the Rising Sun
we shall surely all fly Home.

Yes, in the long ages of Earth time since Lumiere had been on the planet, much had indeed changed. Gone were the high, clear vibrations of the Motherland and all that was before the Fall. Now what remained on Earth would be totally unrecognizable to her, and of such a different frequency from whence she had come. The luminous vibrations of Love that enfolded her in the

Venusian atmosphere dissolved, even as a mist before the morning sun. Was it real…had it all been a dream?

Upon her entry into this lower vibrational dimension, she was overwhelmed with the awareness that all hearts here were closed, to greater or lesser degree, and that the pain of this closure was like a wall of contracted energy, so utterly dense and dark as she had never before known.

As the delicate fibres of her being began to touch the dense vibrational field of Earth, she was struck with an overwhelming sensation of contraction, as if suddenly she had to become very small and closed to fit into such a tight place. This sensation in itself was so uncomfortable, and yet even more so was what arose from her depths… the feelings of unutterable loss and grief with which she had last left this world; it all began to flood into her again…the images, the feelings, all left behind so long ago, all tangled together now as one immense agonizing feeling of loss and separation. Loss of what? Separation from who? Unnameable everything, it seemed…

She had been off the planet for oh, so long… so long…

Slowly her being began to acclimate and her fine, pure essence found its keeping place deep within her innermost recesses. Her remembrance was intact, or mostly so, given the very nature of the density of the Earth now, that caused every soul to slumber and forget who they are.

But her long respite upon Venus, where time did not exist, and consciousness is pristine in clarity, enabled her to retain her soul imprint of who she was, where she had come from, and why. Despite the veils of forgetfulness that would fall upon all who entered this dense realm of Earth, they would not fall so heavy upon her.

She would yet remember who she was.

Thus it was that she and the ones who were to accompany and assist Yeshua were born into the order of the Essenes. The way had been prepared, as the Elders of the Essenes had foreseen their coming. Long ago, across the sands of time, in their homeland of Egypt, there had been etched in the ancient stones there, and in great monuments, now worn with the passing of ages, the signs and symbols that foretold the return of the Light.

Lumiere became a reputed Healer and a beloved apostle of Yeshua, the Anointed One, whom she served tirelessly. She often worked beside him, bringing healing and solace to the people, who had now fallen so far into separation that their lives were fraught with unimaginable pain and sorrow.

The people were ill…in body, mind, heart, and spirit. They were fragmented from their own souls, having forgotten who they are and their connection to Source. They had forgotten the Sacred Ways, the ways of remembrance; indeed they had forgotten everything. Lost, they wandered through this life as if sleepwalking. The perception of separation shaped their reality, and thus they lived in great fear and anguish, lost to the truth of existence.

In this atmosphere, amongst these people, Yeshua walked. He ministered and taught wherever anyone would listen, but not many would, or could. They were sleeping in unconsciousness, and little could they hear the voice of one who spoke from such clear, awakened knowing.

But Love...this he could bring, and the love-starved could receive, if only tentatively at first. For Love transcends all language, crosses all boundaries, breaks down all walls. He ministered a pure Love that none could deny, though many tried. Pure Love is a force that will melt the hardest, most frozen hearts, and eventually it did. And those whose hearts were melted became his followers; like bees to a flower they were drawn irresistibly by the fragrant nectar of his Divine Love.

Blessed one, dear gentle heart...
I am touched by your innocence, your sorrow,
and your longing.
You are but a child there,
beneath those well-worn robes of countless incarnations.
In your tears I see
crystalline reflections of Eternity,
and visions of the Lands of Light
from whence we once did come.
Those tears melt my heart,
and all that is seemingly separate
dissolves into the oneness of this moment
when I take you in my arms
and hold your fragile heart as a precious flower.
Then it is so simple...
there is only one of us here.
One child of Eternity, weeping the only tears
that have ever been wept throughout the ages...
feeling the only pain that all hearts have ever known.
And if I only could, I would take you Home.
I would hold you in my arms, and take you Home...

for it does not seem to me
that we could ever go alone.
You are myself...as all things are...
myriad shimmering fragments
of One Radiant Star...
and our only reason for being is to love
for Love is who we are.

———

As Lumiere tended to the suffering of the many, she came to understand more deeply the human condition, and her heart ached with the greatest tenderness. Feeling the ancient wound that humanity carried, she was overcome with compassion. Many were the broken, worn, and weary ones she held in her arms as they wept. And she fervently prayed that she might ease their pain and lighten their burdens.

But she, too, became weary, as did even Yeshua. They worked together tirelessly for the most part, walking from village to village, sleeping little and often just out in the fields and under the stars, resting seldom, eating little, giving all that they had to those in need. Usually they were a little band traveling together, Yeshua and his faithful disciples.

There was a home in one of the villages where they were often found, and here in the evenings, at the close of the long day's work, they could rest. In the cooler nights they would gather before the great stone hearth, sitting quietly together, gazing into the fire, warming their weary bodies.

Yeshua would sometimes lay his weary head in her lap, with a sigh, his beautiful face illumined in the firelight. And Lumiere would softly stroke his head, running her fingers through his long hair, and giving what healing she could to this One who gave so much to all. These were the sweetest moments to Lumiere…to bring some comfort to the One who comforted so many.

Sometimes, in the heat of the summer, when he sat teaching in the shade beneath the olive trees, the disciples gathered around him, she would quietly lay her head upon his feet. Bathed in his Golden Light, the world, and the weariness of it all, fell away for a time, and she wished these moments to never end. She called him Master; he called her "my little Dove," for she was the purest and gentlest of creatures.

She was here in service to Him and the greater plan that was unfolding. This is why she had come…to once more seed Light into the darkness. Was this not how it had always been? Had she not always served the One Light, to see it prevail upon this planet? She would come again and again for this…they all would, those of the Christ Lineage from Sirius, for this was the blueprint, the design, from the beginning.

And as she walked with Yeshua, tending the suffering of humanity, she felt the depth of this commitment that her soul had always made. Yet, she also felt deep in her own heart the silent ache she herself now carried. An ancient memory stirred there, a dimly veiled feeling of her own loss and separation from an ancient Homeland of long ago and all that she had loved so deeply. There was a quiet yet constant ache of longing within her heart. Longing for what…? For who…?

It would be yet another lifetime before she would remember.

They healed the people with Love, yes, and as the frozen hearts of the suffering people began to thaw and open, they became more receptive to the wisdom teachings that Yeshua imparted. He reminded them of their power, their true power, which is Love…and he reminded them that as they began to love themselves again they would come into their strength and true power. Then they would know how to live in balance in this world, walking with dignity as they themselves could call forth their own power to heal themselves and to live in righteousness.

Yeshua and his disciples shared the wisdom of the Essenes…the knowledge of our interconnectedness with all life, and the pure and simple understanding of respect for the Earth and the natural world. Our bodies are woven of the Earth; therefore we must abide by the laws of the Earthly Mother if we are to remain whole. The angels of the elements: earth, air, fire, water…all these are agents of the Earthly Mother, and as we learn to respect all the elemental forces, we come into alignment with the Circle of Life.

The people were taught how to fast, and cleanse their bodies of the myriad impurities that cause illness, the impurities of wrong eating, wrong living, wrong thinking. And as their bodies were cleansed, they began to feel the Light come into them again, and for perhaps the first time in their lives, felt a joy and gratitude for life.

Ah, gratitude…yes, Yeshua taught this one simple truth: gratitude. The great attitude. When there is gratefulness there is a Great Fullness in the heart, a fullness of love for life, and this is truly our source of happiness.

"Be grateful," he said, *"for this precious gift of life that you have been given. Your Earthly Mother and your Heavenly Father, the Sun, have bestowed you with the miracle of life! Do not take this for granted! Give praise and worship of them!"*

And so the people were taught the Way of the Circle of Life…that as we give our praise to the Source, then does the Source more abundantly give back all that we need, and the circle of giving and receiving is complete. Simple truth this is, indeed, yet forgotten, and so vital and necessary if we are to live in wholeness.

"Rise with the morning Sun and give thanks to your Father of Lights for giving you another day of His glorious Light and warmth, that makes all things under the Sun have life.

Kneel down and touch the Earth with reverence, and give thanks and praise to your Earthly Mother, who has woven our bodies of Her substance and who sustains our bodies with each breath, with each morsel of food, with each step we take upon Her Sacred Body.

Give thanks to the angels of water, blessed life-giving water, so pure and beautiful, without which we could not live! Give thanks to the angels of the air, blessed life-giving air, which is our breath, our life. Oh, give thanks and praise with each and every breath…

And when you receive food, let it be with great thankfulness, for it is made from the hands of the Earthly Mother and the light of the Heavenly Solar Father, and see that it is pure and nourishing as was intended, neither defiled by unnatural processing nor destroyed by the fires of cooking. And eat not the flesh of beasts, for this is not what was intended for you to eat. The creatures are your brothers and sisters upon the Earth, and they are to be loved and cared for, not destroyed and devoured! For if you eat of their flesh, it will make you ill, in body and in soul, for you have transgressed the sacred law of life.

Therefore, eat of the herbs of the Earth, the green growing things, which give you strength, and the fruits and nuts of the trees, which are sweet with the Sun's light, and fall when they are ripe, into your hand, and are given freely. And eating thus, abiding by the laws of the Earthly Mother, you shall know peace, health, and happiness all the days of your lives."

And he taught the worship of the Sun, in the way of the Ancients, and the practice of direct communion with our Solar Source through gazing deeply into its Light at the hours when the intensity was most diffused: sunrise and sunset. This ancient practice allowed great Light to enter the people, healing the eyes first, then the mind and the body. He also taught that this was our original food, our truest nourishment, and that we could indeed live on this nourishment alone and that it would restore our vibrations to their original pristine, Divine blueprint.

Thus Yeshua imparted great wisdom, and those who did listen and abide by what he said became whole again, in body, mind, and spirit.

Beautiful and precious, and yet so brief and fleeting were those days when Yeshua walked amongst the people with his devoted disciples, offering the truth and wisdom of Love's Pure Light. And Lumiere wished it would never end, that he would be always amongst them, always radiating his golden Light and perfect Love. But alas, the time of completion, that was foretold, drew near…

And though there were many who could receive his Love and his Wisdom, and who chose to follow in his ways, there were also many who feared him and despised him. His Light was so pure and so bright that those who chose to abide in darkness were threatened by it and became defensive. In the most hurtful and unconscious ways, they sought to tear him down, and if they could, to make him as small as they themselves felt. They sought to crush his spirit and extinguish his Light, for it shone full upon their own darkness, and they could not bear it. And so, his name was slandered and his character questioned and misrepresented in the most insidious ways, and seeds of mistrust were cast out amongst the people. So that those who could not really feel or see the truth, began to doubt and question who he was and what he taught. And there were whispers amongst the multitudes, hurtful words and destructive criticism were spread around, and generally there was an unrest and a division amongst the people.

The powers that be, those who held positions of power in the government, caught wind of this unrest and these whisperings, and it was only a matter of time before action was taken. Indeed, as is the way of this realm of duality, the Dark rose up against the Light, and was determined to destroy it.

In those final days of Yeshua's embodiment, those who had come with him had been prepared for this time to come and they understood their place and their purpose. This would be the most difficult time: the time they had been chosen for, the Great Initiation. Whatever the appearance of how it would unfold, they must not waver in their ability to hold the Light. Yeshua would need to have sustained for him the immaculate concept of his undying Eternal Self. It would appear he was suffering, that he was dying. But they must know how to look beyond appearances.

Those nearest him had to hold the knowing of the truth. He could not die; he is Eternal Light and Immortal Spirit! If the identification with appearances became stronger than the truth of his Eternal Being, all would fail. He would demonstrate how to break the bond of illusion in matter's spell. But to achieve this, neither he nor they must identify him with his limited, mortal form. This would be the supreme initiation.

Lumiere knew well how to hold the Light unwaveringly. Was this not what she had always done, in this world and beyond? But they were robed in matter now, in human form, and the vibrations were denser than ever she had known before. It was not the pure, high frequency of Venus, nor even of Lemuria long ago. She would have to draw from the deepest reservoir of her soul the knowing of how to hold such light in this darkest of darkness. She must not fail, or all would be lost.

And so it was, that the Keeper of the Temple of Love's Pure Light upon Venus and the High Priestess of the Golden Temple of the Sun of Lemuria remembered…

She remembered.

And all at once, time ceased…space disappeared; past and future collapsed into this One Eternal Moment… where the light of ten thousand suns blazed, and the air crackled as in a great lightning flash…

And thus the Eternal entered Time, and Time was no more...

Then the bonds of Time's prison were broken. Death was defeated. The transfiguration codes were established in matter...

and the gateway of Ascension opened.

It was done. It was fulfilled. And Yeshua was complete in his mission and could go on. Now, he no longer was amongst them in the flesh, and they would each have to rise up into their own divine power and stand in their strength and dignity. Even as he had done, they must also do...so, he had said.

And for those who remained behind, there was yet another daunting task, and that was to keep the Light that he'd anchored in this dimension from being distorted. It was clear that no one of the human kind had understood who he really was and for what purpose he had come. The human politics were complex, and tainted with dark and self-serving behaviour of all manner. The distortion that could occur in his name was an immensely dangerous possibility.

Also, the disciples who had been nearest him were in danger, for the same violence that had been brought upon Yeshua could as easily be directed at anyone who had been in association with him.

So it was that a small group of his closest ones made haste to depart the land in the darkness of night. They would be secreted away in a small trading ship that belonged to a trusted friend of the family who wished to help.

They came ashore in the southern part of a land now known as France. Exhausted and worn from all that had transpired in those last days, they took some rest there by the sea, if only briefly. But they must make haste and find refuge in higher and more hidden ground. Thus they journeyed inland and then made their way into a remote and wild mountainous region of high rocky cliffs and deep valleys. Here they would take refuge. Some would stay here, Lumiere among them, while others would go on into the north and across another sea to distant isles.

It was understood that the essence of the teachings of Yeshua must be kept pure and undistorted and thus hidden, so the seed of Light that he had brought would not wither or be destroyed. Indeed it was foreseen that this would happen, as the religions that would later form around his name and his teachings would be manipulated by powers of greed and corruption.

This tender seed of pure Christ Light must once again, as long ago, be kept safe and protected. It must continue to be nurtured and tended until the time of Harvest. It would be yet some ages before it would come to full flowering, and the fruit of that flowering was to be the fulfilment of Earth's destiny to become a Luminous world, a shining star, whereupon all would be awakened and realized in their divinity.

Thus we know only that Lumiere passed through this way, but all else is veiled in mystery. She disappeared...

and where she went, no one knows. But here in this remote mountainous region of the south of France, the seed of pure Christ Light was planted. And she would be back, in another life, to nurture that seed. It would go on…to flower, and the flowering of that seeding would be a white rose.

Chapter 10
Interlude

She began to awaken, and it was to the touch of a hand softly caressing her brow. The snows were still falling, as they had been for so long. Behind her still closed eyes she saw images of vast mountainous regions, rugged precipices touching the brilliant blue sky, which went on forever, and great winged birds soaring. Rushing streams poured down steep, rocky mountainsides, flanked by meadows of wildflowers. In the distance the high piercing cry of a falcon echoed across the lonely landscape...calling, calling plaintively...

The images shifted to a rich, lush jungle, and she was walking barefoot on velvet green moss forest floors...and a great sphinx moth just above her head spread his giant wings out and fluttered a welcome. Beams of sunlight streamed in golden rays down through the green canopy, and the lone bird cried again...

———

She turned in her dreaming, was blinded once more by a brilliant flash of Light like ten thousand suns, and was lost once more to this world...

Chapter 11
Time and Timelessness

Time...how convincing an illusion it is! Past, future, present...all blur together, like a soft wash of watercolours, and the images once distinct and clear begin to soften, melt, and fade...

What is real?

Is this not all some dream being dreamt by One, who, enjoying slumbering, is in no hurry to awaken? Who then is this Dreamer and who the dream? But One...

The mind expanding from linear realms to spatial awareness collapses Time in a timeless instant, and what once seemed so solid and real disappears like mist before the morning sun.

Looking back, it all does seem just a dream...

But what of those feelings that in this moment, in this life, arise mysteriously from some secret depths to haunt each breath and footfall of our days? Those feelings, that longing, this ancient familiar ache, is not illusion. It's visceral, felt in every fibre and tissue and bone, felt in our souls...

To give voice to the inexpressible mystery of our hearts, and hence find some measure of relief from these ghosts of feelings that haunt our days and nights...for this a story is told.

It is somewhere in the first two decades of the twenty-first century...auspicious time! Or so it is believed... dreamed thus.

A different time, a strange time, a wondrous and challenging time! The world is ending, or being born... no one knows for sure. And life is reeling madly out of control everywhere; sped up, frantic.

Yet in the forest a leaf falls softly, in no hurry, wafting down in a slow, undulating surrender...even as it has for thousands or millions of years. The sun still rises and sets in processional tune with the seasons, and the stars still gaze down with shining, unblinking eyes, as they have forever.

The constellations dance and twirl in the heavens to the music of the spheres; there's Sirius still chasing the mighty hunter Orion, who is chasing the little Fox, who is chasing the Seven Sisters. They're all still carrying on... nothing changes in eternity.

Meanwhile on Earth, in the Dream of time, birth and death appears like a blinking light...here, gone, here, gone, here, gone...and this, too, begins to blur into an unchanging continuum, an unbroken stream of consciousness.

But what of these feelings? To be human is to feel. The stars don't feel, nor the falling leaf, nor the river flowing ever toward the sea, though she sings. To be human is to feel. This is our crowning glory, and this is our crucifixion. And this it is that sets us apart from the stars and the sea. This tender, vulnerable flesh; this excruciatingly sensitive heart, which beats by some mysterious and divine design; that beats humbly and faithfully and carries a life form for countless thousands of beats without stopping, until it does.

What of this heart that gets broken? In every possible way...and isn't it so that not one of us leaves this world with our heart unscarred?

This...it is this. This is the most precious treasure, the jewel beyond measure...this life, these feelings, this pain, this bliss...it all goes on and on and on... this Dream.

It was the strangest time to be upon the Earth: the Harvest time, the end time. Indeed it seemed many lifetimes passed in that one, for time was compressed and convoluted as it sped ever more and more rapidly towards its dissolution.

They had to endure witnessing the dying of the planet, and in the last days felt the death throes of the Mother as Her once verdant forests fell, Her seas darkened, and Her skies filled with strange spider webs of chemicals that turned the once pure blue expanse to a toxic, milky grey. More and more insidious creations came into being...technologies that would manipulate the delicate atmosphere and the subtle energies of the planet, using frequencies of such a distorted nature as to rearrange the perfect order of existence and precious balance of the Earth. The sacred Web of Life was being ruthlessly broken and destroyed.

Yes, dark Alien forces were behind this destruction, having once again, as in the time of Atlantis long ago, infiltrated the planet through a global elite which was secretly taking over this world. Well, secret, that is, only to those who would not open their eyes and see the signs in the skies, and in the Earth and in the eyes of the people who were hypnotized by a mass mind-control.

Giant Corporations now ran the planet, though people blindly refused to acknowledge this, and the intentions of those in power were to dominate the Mother and enslave the people and all life. But who would see…? It was all so covert, yet as evident as looking up and watching the skies being filled with poisons that poured in long trails behind the planes, turning the skies a sickly white. But so much hypnotism and denial made the people blind. They were consumed with consuming in a society gone totally materialistic.

Broken was the sacred Circle of Life…and the people were deeply ill; devoid of true spiritual connection, they were easily persuaded to give their power away to false gods, false religions, and a soulless existence.

Even as their bodies were woven of the Earth, their innocent flesh reflected what She is enduring. Many became very ill, with all manner of diseases, strange distortions of the design of life that was once, in the beginning, created to be perfect. Yet even this became accepted as almost normal, as though sickness and suffering were inevitable, just what happened here. Gone, or mostly gone, was the sacred awareness of the Circle of Life, and the ancient wisdom of the Mother. Her perfect design was broken and forgotten.

It did not rain for long spells, and the Earth became so dry that not even the people's tears could flow. Then it rained endlessly, it seemed, and none could cease weeping. It was fiercely cold and fiercely hot, and the seasons turned all around and inside out. All biology groaned beneath the force of an unprecedented quickening change.

Yes, it was a strange and difficult time upon the Earth, but when, since the Fall, had it not been? The pain, the nightmarish horrors this world has known: untold destruction, wars, hunger, tortures, insanity. Yes, it's all been done or being done, as though the Light has to know the absolute extreme opposite of what it is... to know truly what It Is. For indeed, is it not so, that against the darkest darkness of night are the stars seen to shine most brightly?

Would the consciousness they'd seeded so long ago all be for naught? Would it all be lost now in this eleventh hour? Would all that they'd given their lives for, lifetime after lifetime, prove futile?

The circle goes 'round and history repeats itself. Life-destroying Atlantean technologies are once more in use, and innocent life suffers senselessly at the hand of insanely heartless greed and misused power.

In these strangest of times, perhaps more challenging than all the previous, they came again... the Star-seeded ones: the Sun Gods, the High Priestess and Priest, the Apostle, the Healer, the noble Knight, and the Rose.

All were here, within them, though buried beneath dimensional layers of forgetfulness. Yet moved by secret promptings, subtle guidance, mute but unrelenting feelings, they were carried upon the river of life, not knowing if their streams would converge.

Yet they would be guided by a feeling...a sensing...a glance...amidst the darkness of the darkest times, when the veils of forgetfulness had fallen so heavy upon them; and they would find each other again.

So the circle goes 'round, and the story's been told, which has no final chapter. Lumiere chose to come back again and to endure another round of Earth life, for she knew she would find him. And so she did...

Ah, but life can be cruel; that she should be born so many years before him; for time exists now, as it did not in Mu, and unlike then, what is of Time is now given credence over what is Eternal.

Thus they could not, or would not, be together in this life, but very briefly. Enough so as to ignite the fires of their hearts into an inferno of feelings and burn away the veils that had obscured their memories.

Enough so as to awaken this story...

Long before this tale could ever be told, years before, I was Awakened. It was the beginning of what would be a long series of Awakenings that ripened my soul to remembrance...

I was sleeping under the stars, in a remote place upon the high, lonely cliffs above the sea. It was wintertime and the air was crisp and cold and clear, such that all the stars of the winter's night sky shone as dazzling diamonds.

It was the particular way that the light shone from my Star that night that woke me. I was alone, but I did not feel alone. There seemed to be a soft, otherworldly Presence emanating from my Star that enfolded me in the tenderest embrace; like a lover, long lost, who came in secret to my bed and awakened me in the night with a touch I had nearly forgotten.

All the pain of separation I had ever known in this life melted away, as my heart was ignited with the remembrance of Home and a Love beyond all love.

All night Sirius pulsed to me a Love Song I had waited forever to hear again. It was the Love Song of Creation, wherein all was created and held in the One Heart of perfect Union.

I wept that night, under my Star, for joy and for

sadness. The sadness of being so long apart in the experience of separation, and the joy of the excruciatingly ecstatic relief and bliss of reunion. That night I awoke from the human Dream of separation, of time and space, and the illusion of being an identity apart from the All. I went Home, although my body moved not from that place where I lay alone in the darkness above the sea. In consciousness I was freed to melt as a drop back into the infinite Ocean of Love that is existence Itself.

All through that timeless night I was merged into Eternity, released from the prison of mind's perception of Time. I knew myself to Be. To Be everything, everywhere, all at once.

The Eternal One who is all Love…I was…I AM.

Both Creator and Creation, I AM…for nowhere is there anything but my Self. I felt Myself as the planet, all her lifeforms, and beyond…into the stars and across all space. I knew Myself as the Heart within every beating heart, and as the Creator of all Hearts.

I was…and I AM…One.

———

Four years later, it happened again. One night, once more under the stars, this time in the desert above Tucson, Arizona. But this night I was not alone, and this night I began to disappear.

It was May, and a warm spring night in the desert. My friend Wiona and I were sitting quietly, watching the lights of the city below and the stars above. Before us were two perfectly straight saguaro cacti, that in the dreamy light of the stars looked like two columns of a temple. We were silent mostly, but I mused to my friend, a sensitive Chinese visionary artist, how it resembled a doorway. He nodded, and we were silent again. Then, after some moments, he softly mused, "I just had a vision. It's long ago, in the time of Christ. You are a young girl, and you're standing before a doorway. You turn and you say 'Are you coming?' and then you pass through."

At these words, I suddenly felt the most extraordinary sensation overcome my body. It was as though all of my past, throughout all time, rushed forward, collapsing like a telescope into this present moment.

And then, it seemed a doorway opened in my consciousness…a doorway to the future, and I was going through…

Out into the stars, out across the universe, expanding in consciousness as I went, until I was the stars and the universe, and it was all One Immense Love. Again. And this Love was I and I was That and all was That.

Once again, this Love was who I was…an unspeakable bliss that just rolled in undulating waves through my body, but my body was now so vast…I was the Universe! I was everything, and that everything was Love, and that everything was an ecstatic Bliss that cannot be described.

And yet still I try…

Then Wiona spoke these words, perhaps without even realizing how potently true they were:

"The crystalline structure of your being is beginning to dissolve!"

And I knew what he meant, though not with "my mind," for I had no mind, as such. But my body shuddered, as currents of energy like electricity shot through me, and rivers of tears, rivers of liquid light, flowed from my eyes, melting down my face, melting me down…

And a whispered voice, my own, perhaps, said, "Oh, my God, it's happening!" and I knew something somewhere deep in my cellular memory that I had always known: that this would one day happen.

This was what I'd come here for.

But oh, my God, it was happening now! I was turning into Light…and the Earth was turning into Light, for the vibration was so high and pure it could not maintain physical density.

I experienced that night, for the second time in this life, who I really Am. An indescribable, Infinite Love…and I experienced, with no uncertainty, the fulfilment of my destiny and the destiny of this planet. I experienced our world turn into Light; I witnessed the Ascension of Earth.

My friend, however, was not having the same experience, but nevertheless was so sensitive as to be attuned to what was transpiring. Suddenly he took my hand. "Don't go yet," he pleaded. "Wait for us; wait for the little ones…"

And these words struck me as very strange and funny, for where could I possibly go? I was Everything, Everywhere, all at once!

Yet I heard, from deep down within the lower dimensions, his plaintive plea echoing, as if it were the voice of all of the children of the Earth who yet were not ready and could not yet come through this doorway.

And so, as the Cosmic Mother of Infinite Love Herself, I turned to him and smiled, a smile of immense compassion and understanding. A smile that said, "Of course, my dear, for you I will do whatever you ask." For Love can only say yes. And slowly, I began to come back.

It was not until several months later, when next we met again, that he told me what he had experienced and witnessed that night. "You were disappearing," he said, "going invisible, dematerializing," and he became alarmed as he watched first my feet, than halfway up my legs dissolve into nothingness. It was at this point that he reached out to call me back. On my part, I did not know I was disappearing…I only knew an ever-expanding bliss that just kept expanding in waves of ecstatic Love…as the One who is…All That Is.

I did come back; from across the universe, all that I am coalesced once more into this small physical form, gradually vibrating once again slow enough to stay in physical matter.

It took many months to integrate back into this dimension. I walked between worlds, here and yet not here, as one who had gone over a threshold of no return, and yet did return. Or so it seems…

And I did not comprehend, with my mind, fully what had happened. Not sure if I do even still. But my heart remembers Union, and this can never be forgotten. I have surmised that I had gone into a future timeline that night, a time out of time, and a future unfolded before my awareness of the promise of fulfilment of a long-held dream destined to be realized. I was Awake as the One Being, God incarnate. And our planet had Ascended.

※

But I had to come back, because it was not yet time…in the realms of Time.

"Yet a little while longer
must the children of Earth dream"

was the message that I was given as I returned back into this dimensional reality.

And I had to come back to bring that higher frequency of purest Love into this dimension, to assist in the ripening of consciousness on this planet, to walk through my destiny as an awakener, and to unwind some last threads of ancestral karma acquired by taking Earth embodiment.

And I had to come back…to find Golden.

It has already happened…it's happening…and it will happen. The Light we'd seeded from the beginning of this world, and held for untold ages, will prevail. We succeeded; the Ascension codes had been established after all. I experienced it, taken as I was through that doorway into the future.

The Light has prevailed. It is already done.

Golden, my beloved, this story is for you. Wherever you are, may you feel the thread of Light I hold for you, as you continue to unwind the layers of karmic patterning that accumulated in your myriad lifetimes of service upon the Earth.

And may you hear me whispering your name to our Star, as I walk alone in the night, remembering.

May you feel my love, that was never born and never dies, for we are and have ever been…One.

About the Author

Grace is an Essene mystic and internationally known healer, spiritual teacher, and mystic poet. For nearly thirty years she has shared her deep heart wisdom, healing presence, and loving guidance with people all over the world. She resides in Mt. Shasta, California.

Made in the USA
Columbia, SC
13 March 2018